CONTROL

TREASURE: 2

JESSA JAMES

Control: Copyright © 2020 by Jessa James

All Rights Reserved. No part of this book may be reproduced or transmitted in any form or by any means, electrical, digital or mechanical including but not limited to photocopying, recording, scanning or by any type of data storage and retrieval system without express, written permission from the author.

Published by Jessa James
James, Jessa
Control

Cover design copyright 2020 by Jessa James, Author
Images/Photo Credit: Deposit photos: Yafimik; SSilver

Publisher's Note:
This book was written for an adult audience. The book may contain explicit sexual content. Sexual activities included in this book are strictly fantasies intended for adults and any activities or risks taken by fictional characters within the story are neither endorsed nor encouraged by the author or publisher.

This book has been previously published.

GET A FREE BOOK!

Join my mailing list to be the first to know of new releases, free books, special prices and other author giveaways.

http://freehotcontemporary.com

1

KATHERINE

I sprint as fast as I can, away from the cops that are pursuing me. Toward what, I don't know. Running towards the two sagging warehouses, placed side by side.

My heartbeat sounds thunderous in my own ears.

Ka-thump.

My muscles are moving me forward, but my arms and legs protest with every step.

Ka-thump.

My mind races, trying to put together a puzzle for which I don't have all of the pieces. There's not a lot of coherent thought going on, just a bunch of reacting based on pure instinct.

Ka-thump.

I reach the bottleneck, where the two warehouses eclipse me. My movement is hidden from anyone behind me. I run through the narrow gap, continuing to the right. I see a partially open door just twenty yards ahead of me. My lungs are screaming for me to stop now, so I sprint to the door, ducking inside.

As soon as I get inside, I miss the dusky light. In here, it's dark and dank and moldy, and my eyes take a moment to adjust. The warehouse is full of old crates and boxes, stacked four times as tall as I am.

I need to move. Standing here like this, I'm a sitting duck. Three avenues open up between the boxes, forcing me to decide which one to take. I choose the left, moving as quickly and quietly as possible down the row of boxes that tower overhead.

There are some paths created by the boxes, here and there where a stack randomly ends and there is a gap before the next begins. I soon see that there are not just the three avenues, but actually a whole network of corollary pathways.

Darting right, off the main path, I work my way through the maze. As I go, I have to slow down because the paths that I travel are getting smaller and smaller, nearly trapping me amongst the towering boxes.

I start to get the same claustrophobic feeling that I felt earlier in the SUV begin to rise. If I die in here, the cops could just leave my body among the boxes and no one would probably even notice.

That is assuming that anyone would even look for me.

Based on the fact that my closest brother, Tony, just sold me to the cops who are pursuing me now, I seriously doubt that.

I clutch at my chest and refuse to let these thoughts settle in my mind. Not when there is so much else at stake.

I reach what seems to be the center of the maze, and realize the main problem with being among the boxes. There isn't anywhere to hide here.

I stop, looking at the heavy cardboard box to my right, examining it for a way in. I find a seam, tracing it around the box with my fingers. But I would have to break into the box to get inside.

I glance up at the towering stack of boxes above it, biting my lip. There is no way of knowing that the box at the bottom wouldn't collapse, trapping me inside. And that's only if I managed to get inside, without any tools to help.

"Hey, in here!" comes a man's voice. Although the voice is a bit distant, I recognize it as belonging to one of the cops. "She could've run in through this open door."

Shit. They are coming my way, it's only a matter of time. I look around, crazed. I have to start moving, that much is for certain.

I decide to move further toward the back of the warehouse, thinking there might be an exit or at least somewhere I can hide back there. In my rush to move quickly, I knock one of the stacks of boxes with my shoulder so hard that it actually rocks back and forth for a second.

Recoiling, I dart away from the boxes, praying that they don't actually fall. I hadn't considered that possibility yet, but I don't want to alert the cops that I'm inside this particular warehouse. Knocking some of these giant boxes to the ground will definitely do that, at the very least.

Far behind me, I hear one of the cops curse, and I get the sense that he just figured out that the boxes are moveable too.

As I go, the pathway gradually opens up. I rush down the widening corridor, trying to make out what lies at the other end. My breathing sounds ragged and harsh to my own ears.

I silently pray that no one else can hear my breaths. I keep going, moving by willpower alone, and then, suddenly, I am running out of the maze.

I look left and right; on the left, at the far end, there

appear to be a set of double doors. In front of me, there is a second floor of what appear to be offices. On my far right, there are stairs that lead up to the second floor.

I race for the exit, ignoring a rat as it scurries across my path. I pump my arms and legs, sprinting flat-out towards the doors. There is graffiti all along the walls here, all red and black, the artist practicing their tag over and over again.

"Skinx", it says. "Skinx. Skinx. Skinx. Skinx. skinx."

I can hear the cops yell to each other as they navigate the maze. I can't tell exactly what they are saying, because their voices are muffled by all the cardboard, but I know that they're still in pursuit.

I make it to the double doors, only to find them padlocked shut, a locked chain entwined between their individual push-to-open handles. I push on one door anyway, feeling panic rising again. It opens a quarter of an inch before the chain pulls tight.

Shit! I bang the door with my hand, only wincing afterward at the noise. I need another escape route, or at least a hiding place.

I glance behind me, then to my right. I don't want to be locked in here, but it looks like I don't have a choice. I start running toward the other end, focusing all my energy on the ratty looking set of metal stairs that lead up to the second floor.

My lungs burn as I reach them. I clatter up the first few before I realize how loud I'm being. Glancing into the forest of boxes, I slow my pace, hoping that I haven't already given myself away.

Every slow step is gut-wrenching. I creep up the stairs on silent feet, taking off running the second I hit the landing. One of the offices is right in front of me, the door left carelessly ajar, and I scramble inside. I close the door behind me, but the door only swings three-quarters of the way shut.

I glance around, trying to get my bearings. There is a large plate glass window right behind me, part of the wall of the office. I don't care, though. At least this way, I'm not as horribly exposed as I was on the stairs. I look around the office, which is filled with dozens of stacks of small boxes. I spy a desk back behind all the boxes.

Bingo. I can hide there.

Crouching low to avoid being seen, I make my way between the stacks, finding the desk in the far right corner. It's made of musty old wood, leaning terribly under the weight of the boxes stacked on top of it. It looks as though it may collapse at any moment, but that doesn't matter to me.

I gladly get on my knees and scramble underneath it, grateful for the cover it provides. I get a charley horse on my thigh as soon as I stop moving, my body protesting all the sudden activity of the last hour.

I massage my leg as best I can, sitting and straining my ears for the sounds of the cops. I try to breathe as regularly as I know how while my mind whirls desperately.

Is it possible that they will just give up, figuring that maybe they had the wrong warehouse? Can I please, please get one single break in this day of horrors?

When I hear the faint clatter of boot steps on the stairs, I swallow. I should've known that I'm not that lucky. I squeeze my eyes shut for a second, fighting back the tears that prick my eyes.

There is no time for tears, not right now. I slap a hand over my mouth, terrified that if I make a sound, they will know just where to find me.

Thunk, thunk, thunk...

I listen to the sound of heavy boots leaving the metal

stairs, prowling in my direction. Shivers begin to wrack my body as the sounds grow closer and closer.

"In here, Hunt," one of them says, just outside the office. "Look at how the dust has been disturbed, here and here."

"Could've been whoever tagged downstairs."

"You ever knew a tagger who explored any area without leaving a mark?" The cop chuckles.

There is the long, sad sighing creak of the office door being opened.

"You ought to come out right now!" the cop calls to me. "We're not going to hurt you unless we have to."

No, you're just going to sell me on to some crazy person. A person who believes that they can and should own people.

I clamp my mouth shut, trying to squelch the bitter tears that threaten to overwhelm me. Huddling under the desk, I pray to God, even though I don't believe in him.

Please. Please, if you're listening... save me. Please!

I jump as the cops overturn one of the stacks of boxes.

"Come on!" the same voice calls. "Don't make me hunt for you! Just get out here!"

"She's not in there," the other cop says, his tone bored.

"Yes, she is." The voice grows closer and closer. "And she had better come out if she knows what's good for her."

I can't move. I can't breathe. I can't think.

All I hear are the footsteps, circling, ready to jump on the slightest sign of life.

"Let's check some of the other rooms up here, man." The cop sounds impatient. "We don't have all day to deliver the girl. I have shit to do."

There is a long pause. I sit there, terrified, while the cop tries to make a decision. Then a dissatisfied male sigh.

"Yeah, okay."

The footsteps start to recede. I am so relieved that I almost let out a whoosh of breath. I shift a little to my left, and the desk creaks loudly.

The footsteps pause. There is a muttered curse.

"I fucking told you she was in here," the cop says. "I fucking told you!"

Their footsteps fly my way. I close my eyes, shivering convulsively, unable to watch the cop search for me. He grabs my arms, dragging me out from under the desk. My eyes pop open as he hauls me upright.

"You fucking stupid bitch," he hisses, triumphant. "You are going to regret ever running from us. We are going to make sure that you are sold to a buyer who makes you beg for your death."

I see the other cop approaching, a syringe at the ready. I open my mouth to reply, although what am I supposed to say? Instead, I just start blubbering, making incoherent sounds.

"Get her right here, in the arm," the first cop says, holding my arm out.

The officer jabs me in the arm, a quick pinprick of pain. Everything starts to blur, the whole world around me losing shape.

"Should've dosed her right off," one of them murmurs.

And then everything goes black.

2

KATHERINE

I wake slowly, realizing that I am lying face down, resting on something hard. I push myself up on shaky arms, looking around the space I find myself in. I'm on the floor of the room, my body heat being seeped away by the cool cement. I try to focus.

I'm in a small bedroom of sorts, with a cot, a scratchy gray wool blanket, and a bucket. Everything is dreary and gray, the same color as the cinder block walls. There is no window in the whole space, which can't be more the eight feet by eight.

It's a jail cell, I realize. I'm in a jail, and no one knows or cares that I am here.

That thought swirls around in my head, but I can't hold onto it. I can't hold onto anything for too long, which is okay with me right now.

The world is still fuzzy, which I blame on the drugs the cops gave me. Whatever I was injected with, has left a bitter tang in my mouth, and makes even my bones feel weak. I sit up, noticing that my pale pink dress is gone, replaced with a starchy grey shift dress, the material prickling my bare skin.

My bra is gone too, which means that someone saw me all but naked when they changed my clothes. I check for my panties, and I'm relieved to find that I'm still wearing the same slip of white satin as before.

At least there is that.

I get to my feet, my whole body aching from running for my life yesterday. My bare feet protest the most. I can feel fresh blisters that have sprouted all along where my toes were in contact with my shoes and the pads of my feet.

I limp over to the cell-like door, pressing my hands against the flat metal. There is a slot halfway down the door, just six inches by three. I bend down to look through it, my body protesting. On the other side, as far as I can see, there is just a stretch of bare wall.

"Hello?" I call out. "Hello? Anyone?"

Silence is the only answer, and it is deafening. I turn around, facing my tiny cell. My brain is still mushy, which keeps me from pondering the worst parts of my situation.

The look on Tony's face just before the cops hauled me away. Guilt, anxiety, maybe just a little bit of smugness.

My father, who apparently, sold me to an unknown buyer. I can't even unpack those feelings without feeling enraged, so it's better to just leave them be.

The future shrouded in mystery.

Where will I be going?

Who will I meet there?

Will I even survive very long?

College is seeming like a faraway dream right now.

Instead, I spend the next few hours learning every inch of my cell. I trace the seams of the cinder blocks. I pull the cot away from the wall, finding a spot in the corner where somebody chipped out a pocket in the floor with some kind of tool. I fold and refold the blanket, searching it for hidden mysteries.

I realize about two hours later, that I have to pee. Like, really, really badly. I call out the door's slot for a while, but there is no response.

With no one coming to my aid and my bladder about to burst, I am forced to use the bucket. I squat over it, hovering, and relieve myself. There is no toilet paper or anything, so I am forced to let myself drip dry.

Then I lie down on the cot, shivering and afraid. Eventually, the hazy effects of the drug are gone from my system. I draw the wool blanket around my frame, shaking. But the wool only keeps out the cool air; it can't keep out the thoughts that threaten to overwhelm me.

The mysterious future. Tony. My father and the rest of my family. Will anyone even know that I've been kidnapped?

These thoughts, and variations thereof, repeat and repeat until I'm a sobbing, crazed mess. Then I cry myself out. I sleep for a while. I wake and remember where I am. The cycle begins again.

Stress. Cry. Sleep.

A whole day passes without any sign of life from outside my door. At one point, I sit by the door and yell for someone to come, but no one does. Not even when my belly starts to cramp with hunger

It's only at the beginning of the third day that I hear heavy boots coming down the hallway, toward my cell.

I scramble off the cot, holding the wool blanket close.

"Hello?" I say, putting my eye to the slot.

Straining to look down the hall, I can see the shape of a large man dressed all in black heading my way. I stare at him, at his bald head, at his beady eyes, and the grim expression on his mouth, at the rigid, unyielding set of his shoulders. If I saw him on the street, I would cross to the other side to avoid him. But he's a person, and I haven't seen a person in three days.

When he approaches my door, I don't know whether to be more excited or frightened. He doesn't say anything as he unlocks my door and swings it open.

"Come," he says simply, gesturing for me to leave the cell. I realize that he's Russian, or maybe Polish or Ukrainian, just from the way he speaks.

"Where are we?" I demand, shivering with a mixture of cold and fear.

"You no talk," he orders, moving toward me. "Just go out."

I look at him for a second, wondering if I should resist him. Then again, what am I really resisting? I have no idea where I am now or where he is supposed to lead me to.

"Just tell me where I am—" I plead.

He cuts me off by grabbing me by the shoulder. He inserts a thumb into the flesh there, digging painfully into my skin until I cry out and begin to shrink from his touch. I reach for him, my fingernails finding purchase in his meaty forearm, but he doesn't even blink in reaction.

"Move!" he yells, giving me a shake.

He rips the wool blanket away with his free hand as he shoves me out of my cell and into the long, sterile hallway. The hallway is shockingly white, broken up only here and there by doors to other cells.

He starts to propel me forward down the hallway. The white tile underfoot is as cold as the cement floors, and it shows some aging, the tiles chipped and cracked.

What is this place? How many other people have been kept here? I count at least six other cells as I am frog-marched past them, but they are all empty.

At the end of the hallway, my guard leads me to a painted white stairwell. I'm half-dragged down the stairs, flight after flight, each flight looking the same as the hallway I just left behind. Six flights, or seven... I lose count of them quickly.

"Where are you taking me?" I try again, but my guard only scowls.

When we reach the bottom floor, he opens the door and pushes me inside. I'm faced with another long hallway of cells, but this one is different.

Though I can't see anyone, these cells are full of people. Women's voices. Some calling out for help, some crying, some just murmuring quietly.

"You go," my guard says, pushing me forward. "Third on right, that is yours."

I drag my feet, trying to see through the tiny slots in the grey doors, but all I can make out are a couple pairs of eyes. My guard has no interest in the moans or pleas coming from the cells; it is almost as though he is immune to them somehow. He hurries me along, swinging the door to my cell open.

"Go in," he says. "You get *nekkid*."

"Please—" I try, only to have his hand descend onto my shoulder again. This time, when he pushes his thumb into my flesh, he does some serious damage.

I cry out, falling to my knees, tears springing to my eyes. While I'm stunned, he leaves, slamming the door shut behind him.

"Wait!" I call after him. "Please wait!"

But he is gone. I crawl on my hands and knees to the door, peering out the slot. Like before, it is made so that I can only see white walls. I can hear plenty, but nothing really sticks out.

"Hello?" I call. "Can anyone hear me?"

If the other women can, they don't respond to me directly. I sink down, despondent.

Mostly, I'm wondering, what now? Why am I here? What is about to happen?

Not too long after my guard leaves, a tiny old Asian woman opens my door. Scowling at me, she holds a fancy white dress on a hanger in one hand and a little, o zippered pouch in the other.

I sit up, studying her face. "Can you tell me where we are?"

If she speaks English, she doesn't care to answer. Instead, she just motions to the shift dress I'm wearing. "Off!"

"Please, where are we?" I say, imploring her.

The woman looks nonplussed and sets the little pouch down.

"Off now!" she says, raising her voice.

"No!" I argue.

A taser appears from the woman's voluminous skirts. She brandishes it, impatient with me. "Off!"

I bite my lip, gauging the distance between me, her, and the door. She sees me looking and steps more fully between me and the door. She rattles the hanger.

I wouldn't have made it anywhere even if I had tried. I know that.

"Off!" she repeats, her tone growing panicky. She glances over her shoulder. I realize that maybe isn't here of her own free will either.

I turn my back on her and pull the shift up over my head. The woman tsks, turning me around. I shiver and try to use my hands to cover my nakedness. I am extremely ashamed, but my red cheeks do nothing to give the woman pause.

She just puts the taser back in her skirts and motions for me to put my hands up over my head. I lift my hands up, and she slips the dress off of the hanger, forcing it down over my head.

I help work the white tulle dress down over my body, dropping its full skirt to the floor. It is a stunning dress; I feel stupid wearing it, not having showered or shaved for three days.

I want to ask what I am being dressed up for, but the more time I spend with this woman, the less convinced I am that she knows anything at all.

The woman grabs the little pouch that she dropped on the floor, unzipping it to reveal a basic makeup kit. She says something in her native tongue, motioning for me to be still. I close my eyes as she dabs some silver eye makeup on my face with her fingers, then does a lot of bright pink blush with a long brush.

When she's done, she looks at me, appraising me. She gives a decisive nod, then turns to leave.

"Wait—" I say, but she doesn't, shutting the door behind her.

Instead, my guard reappears, a syringe in his hand. My eyes widen as I realize that I'm going to be dosed again, and I struggle as he grabs me.

"No! No, I don't want that!" I cry. "No, please—"

He injects me in my upper arm, ignoring my struggles. Instead of everything going black though, the world just seems to soften. The light takes on a golden hue and my interest in resisting...

Whatever that was, it's gone now.

My guard leads me out of my cell by the arm, and I go, utterly docile.

3
ARSEN

As my two enforcers ride in the front seats, I sit in the back seat of the SUV, my fingers tented. I stare pensively out the window. After a wild three days of almost nonstop negotiating and threatening, I've finally managed to find her.

Katherine Carolla, the wretched daughter of Sal Carolla.

See, Sal wouldn't give up his daughter's location, even when my booted foot was on his neck, my gun pointed to his temple. I admit I was in a little bit of awe of him, of that kind of stubborn protectiveness. Of course, I killed him anyway, but I still admired it.

Then I found out that the real reason old Sal wouldn't fess up to hiding pretty little Katherine is that he *sold* her to a very exclusive private auctioneer.

He *sold* her.

Like she wasn't his daughter. As if she was just an asset to him, and he was just biding his time, keeping her hidden until he could profit from her unveiling.

When I found out, I was so surprised I actually laughed out loud.

As it turns out, little Katherine wasn't being protected by her daddy after all. Her daddy was protecting someone who Sal *knew* would dress up his daughter and sell her to the highest bidder. A person whom, it was assumed, would rape her thousands of times. Or pass her around to his friends, maybe.

Or just plain kill her.

If I was capable of feeling such a thing, I would almost feel sorry for Kathrine.

Almost.

Too bad she was a Carolla. She would be made to pay, as Anna had paid. Except I had bigger plans for Katherine...

Plans that involved breaking her, body and soul. Using a special blend of physical labor, torture, and sex to brainwash her. To torment her into thinking whatever I want her to think.

She hasn't even laid eyes on me yet, but her mind and body are *mine*.

Then I can trot her out at strategic intervals, namely, to scare the shit out of my rivals. My perfect little pet, all dark and twisty. I get a little hard right here in the car, just thinking about ruining her body, crushing her spirit.

My enforcer Denis pulls into a gated area that surrounds what looks like a beige airplane hangar, closed on all four sides. The building is isolated from everything else, no structure is even close to it. Denis pulls up to a security checkpoint, presenting my invitation to the auction to the armed guard.

An invitation that I had to pull in several favors to receive.

The guard looks at me, looks at Denis and Roget, and

then waves us through. A valet attendant directs us to pull up at an unmarked door. I get out of the car, stretching a little bit. I look at my two enforcers, who are scanning the entire parking lot and the entrance for threats.

I consider myself tall and broad, at a little over six feet. Denis and Roget are fucking enormous though, each six and a half feet tall and built like twin lumberjacks.

Well, if lumberjacks dressed in trench coats and were armed to the fucking teeth, that is.

"This way, gentlemen, if you will?" a man says, bowing as he opens the door.

I lead the way inside, blinking at the darkness. We step into a small space, lit only by a heavy-duty flashlight.

"Gentlemen, if you will find a mask?" the man says, gesturing to a table full of identical black face masks.

Roget grabs three masks, and I take mine from him. After he and Denis slide their masks on, I pull mine on as well. We all look at each other, at the almost comical erasure of our most distinguishing features.

"Grim," Denis says. Roget just grunts and adjusts his heavy jacket.

"Right this way," the man says, sweeping a door open and motioning inside. "You're among the last to arrive. I'm afraid we will have to seat you near the back."

That wasn't a miscalculation on my part; I want to be in the back, engulfed in shadows. The man hurries in front of me, his footsteps light on the bare concrete. He leads the way into the main room, trying to be respectful of the fact that the show has already started.

About fifteen men stand in little clumps, their attention glued to the girl being led up onto a raised platform by a masked man in black. The girl is wretched, her skin sallow and her bones all but showing through her dress. She's also high as a fucking kite, her eyes large and glassy, her mouth so dry it's cracked in a few places.

"This is Selina... She starts at $10,000..." the man announces in a high-pitched voice.

Immediately, two hands shoot up.

"Alright, I've got twelve thousand..." the man says.

More hands go up.

I relax a little, rolling my shoulders. I'm not here for just any girl, so I can tune out the bidding war. All I have to do is not become impatient and lose my temper with anyone here before Katherine Carolla is called up.

Easy enough, as long as the other men keep their distance.

While I wait, I bide my time by thinking about the girl.

Katherine.

I hate that name. One of the first things I'm going to do is make her wear my chains...

And the second thing is to rename her. Something more fitting to her new station.

Like Slave. Or Servant.

My lips curve upward in the cruelest secret smile.

I'm going to take her to my compound, far away from here. There, I can do whatever I want, whenever I want. I am like a king on my compound.

Then I'm going to enjoy slowly breaking her bones and swiftly crushing her spirit. Let her know that I have killed her family; let her know that no one is coming to save her. When she weeps for her father and brothers, I will whip her for caring that they existed.

I tighten my fists. It is her fault for being born a Carolla. Her fault that they are all dirty, tainted fucking losers.

Scratch that... *were* losers. I've pretty much ticked every one of them off my list of people to kill. I eviscerated each one of the bastards back there in the warehouse, and I did it with a smile.

Their dead eyes stared back at me as I laughed. They all learned not to fuck with what I call mine...

I picture Anna, her mouth open in a surreal display of surprise. Even if she was just some whore, she was still *my* whore. *My* property. *Mine*.

I push the memory down. There are other things to focus on, like the way it will sound when I snap the cuffs closed on Katherine's wrists. I focus on that, tuning out the bidding for the next girl, and the next.

Of course, I will have to buy Katherine. A lot of money, if these sad looking girls are anything to judge by.

And because she made it so difficult for me to find her, she is going to really suffer. Much more than if she'd simply been present the day I murdered her family.

A thought comes into my head.

A confession. I could make her sign a confession, of her own free will. Owning up to everything that her family did that displeased me, including Anna's death.

That would be fun.

After I've stripped her of her will to live, she will beg me for the release that death brings. Just like the others did.

And then I'll choke her, slowly. I will be the one to see the light leave her eyes, see her entire being flicker out of existence.

That moment... that moment will be so, so sweet.

Across the room, the dull brunette slave currently being auctioned off collapses. No one overreacts, which is kind of strange. The auctioneer just calls the last bidder the winner, while another burly man in a mask comes and gathers the girl up, throwing her over his shoulder almost carelessly.

"Katherine is our next girl," the auctioneer buzzes. "Bring out Katherine."

I sit up a little straighter. A petite blonde is guided out onto the platform, her delicate features enhanced by her white dress. She leans her head back to look around, her head wobbling.

It's her.

She's pretty, in a delicate sort of way. Large expressive eyes, a full mouth, high cheekbones. What is so striking to me is that she looks like Anna, my favorite whore in New Orleans. There is a similarity around the eyes, and a sort of wisdom that is out of place on someone her age.

It makes me wonder what Katherine has seen. It makes me wonder too what Anna saw, in her brief years on this planet. That thought makes me tense up and makes me grit my teeth. I feel the impressions of my nails biting into the palms of my hands as I clench my fists. Denis nods to her with a questioning look, and I nod back.

That's the girl we came here for. That's the girl we're going to be leaving with, no matter what.

She's very young. I study her. Her frail arms, her small tits. Her face, sort of elven in quality, with big blue eyes, an upturned nose, full wide lips.

Oh, the things I plan to have those lips do. She surveys the room with those blue eyes of hers, but her face gives nothing away.

I realize with a start that she's not terrible looking, not even standing front and center in that hand-me-down dress. That doesn't really matter to me, but it doesn't hurt, either.

Fuck, I am a man, after all.

The man holding her up is doing a shitty job, letting her fall halfway over. Clearly, she's on the same drug as the rest of the girls. She'd better not fucking pass out, not before I buy her.

I want her to remember the feeling of being treated like a piece of property.

"Young Katherine is still a virgin," the auctioneer calls. His words hit me like a ton of bricks. A virgin? That will likely double her price. "She belonged to Sal Carolla. Now she can belong to you."

Several men cheer, ready to claim their prize. But those men don't realize that I am in the audience, or that I am who I am, or that I'm here for *her*.

I start to move forward, cupping my hands around my mouth. "One million. One million, and we're done."

Everyone turns and looks at me, some seeming surprised.

"One million, from this gentleman," says the auctioneer. "Do I hear—"

"One and a quarter," calls a man across the way. He smirks at me.

"One and a half," I say.

"Two million!" says the man. "Two million dollars."

"Three," I growl.

The man hesitates, looking at the two men who are with him. One of them nods to him, and he grins. "Three point five."

"Four million," I call out, even though it is a stunning amount of money.

Money is no object, not today.

The other man pulls out his gun, though what he plans to do with it I'm not certain. He makes the deadly mistake of looking as though he might be aiming at me, and the next thing I know, I have my gun drawn.

Instinct takes over, slowing things down for me.

Everyone ducks for cover. Soon there is a bullet hole neatly between his eyes. My gun smokes just a little.

Everyone else begins to move. The sound of dozens of guns being cocked rings loudly in the still air. Denis and Roget are at my side, though obviously, I don't need them.

"Call it," I command the auctioneer. "Call it now, and we can leave."

The auctioneer puts his hands up, though I'm not pointing my gun at him. "Sold?" he squeaks uncertainly.

The masked man that holds Katherine upright pulls her down off the platform, heading toward a back room with her trailing limply. I gesture for Denis to go get her, excitement welling up in my chest.

Everyone is on tenterhooks, watching my every movement, guns at the ready. But I'm not concerned with any of them.

No, I'm concerned with my new purchase, who Denis rips away from her guard. As he leads her over to me, I realize just how small she is beside my enforcer. She can't be much more than five feet tall.

They reach the spot where I'm standing, and I look at her wide, desperate eyes, her blonde hair, her hands knotted in her white dress. It's all much more than I dreamt of. More real, more vivid.

I cock my head and give her a considering glance. "You belong to me. I am your master now."

There is a faraway echo of terror in those big blue eyes, but whatever drug she's been given prevents her fear from rising to the surface.

Not for long, though. When I get her back to my compound, there will be no substances, nothing between us. Nothing to stop her from feeling the kind of terror that Anna felt in her last hours.

I feel like I should warn her, let her know what sort of master I will be. I dig in my pocket for my switchblade, popping its shining blade open.

Her eyes fill with a distinct note of fear as I brandish it, stepping closer to her. I grab her by the shoulder, enjoying her pathetic attempts to struggle. Denis steps forward and grabs both of her hands, pulling them behind her back.

I look her right in the eyes as I slowly slice the letter A into her collarbone, about an inch by a half an inch. I get hard when she lets out a plaintive wail. My fingers shake with pent-up excitement as her blood trickles out over my knife.

Nothing has ever felt so good, I swear.

"This is to remind you that you belong to me," I tell her, wiping the blood off of my blade on her perfect white dress, right on her right breast. The blood spreads and seeps immediately, which is very satisfying.

I turn on my heel, ready to go. I look at Denis. "All right. Put the bag over her head, and we can go. We have a long journey ahead of us."

Then I make my way out of the airplane hangar, ripping my face mask off and tossing it to the ground.

4

KATHERINE

I have a vague memory of being injected with tranquilizer a few times. I remember being awake enough to recognize a plane and a car. I know that the man that taunted me after he bought me was nearby that whole time.

I see him in my mind. His strange grey eyes and his dark brow, his large frame and black clothing, the dark stubble on his cheeks. His skin isn't the same tone as mine... it was more olive in complexion. When he spoke, his English was accented...

But I was too far gone from the drugs to determine any more than that.

I wake again, coming fully into consciousness, and I look up at a royal blue ceiling. I groan to myself, leaning up to look down at my body. Gone is the dress that I wore at the auction. In its place is a deep, blood red sleeveless shift dress.

My fingertips accidentally brush a spot on my collarbone and even that slight touch stings. Carefully, I pull my dress away from my skin, peering down at a smoothly bandaged spot about an inch by an inch. It's then that I remember his expression when he dug his knife into my flesh, the glee I saw in his eyes when he marked me forever.

Even though I am careful not to disturb the spot further, I have to struggle against the tears that prick my eyes. What kind of monster just outright mutilates another human being?

To my utter humiliation, my panties and bra are gone too. I feel naked, knowing that someone looked at my completely nude body while I was unconscious.

My shoulder throbs, reminding me of that moment back at the auction, when he showed me who he was by carving something into my flesh. I lift my hand to touch the spot that he marred with his knife. A gentle clanking draws my attention to my wrist, where I find a finely wrought handcuff attached to a delicate-looking gold chain.

I tug on the chain and find that I'm tethered to some place behind the bed. I have enough chain to move around the room, but not enough to go anywhere outside the room.

This is... bizarre. Where exactly am I? I know it's the daytime, but I have no other clues.

Then I think about where my family is, and it all sort of hits me at once.

Gone, that's where my family is. They've left me, intentionally. I'm not the kid from *Home Alone*, I'm Liam Neeson's daughter in the movie *Taken*.

Worse, I've been *sold*.

Just what am I supposed to do with that information? As tears start to well in my eyes, I can't help but see the events of the last few days play out in my head.

Tony's expression when he betrayed me to the cops.

The cop's face when he hauled me out from underneath the desk.

The horrible misery that I faced when I woke up in my cell at the auction house.

And *him*. The man who bought me. His eyes... the cruelty and derision I saw there gave me chills.

I roll onto my side, my tears escaping onto the grey fabric under my body. What could I have done to drive my family to sell me? Sobbing, I think of Tony's warning.

Did Dad really sell me because he was running out of money? Could I really be worth so little to them?

Don't they love me?

Snot runs from my nose, and I wipe at it with a corner of my shift dress. I let my tears overwhelm me for a little while, crying until I feel completely hollow inside.

No one comes to the dark wood door at the sound of my tears; there isn't anyone here that is very interested in whether or not I am comfortable, I know that for sure.

I blink a few times, looking at the large bed I am in. There are no sheets or blankets, just a soft grey cover over the entire thing. The room itself is pretty large, with no decoration except a window seat built into a bay window. There is no cushion, and the window has no drapes or dressing.

I scoot myself off the bed, standing on my wobbly legs. The floors are all dark wood, smooth and cool against the pads of my bare feet. I go to the door first, but find it locked.

Unsurprising, I guess. After all, I am chained up. It's not like I could leave if I found the door open.

Next, I explore the other side of the room, going to the window seat. The window is thick double-paned glass, and it doesn't open. Outside the window is shockingly picturesque; I'm high up, overlooking a small orchard in full bloom. Behind that is a crumbling brick wall, with lush greenery and mountainous terrain. Everywhere that I can see in the distance is just hills upon hills, jungles on top of jungles.

Wherever I am, I am definitely not in New Orleans anymore.

That brings on another crying jag, even though I still feel empty from earlier. This one isn't quite so energetic, more just weeping quietly while staring out the window.

Though I'm distraught, I realize that I'm hungry. I'm not really sure what to do about that. I try to remember my last real meal, and I can only think of the morning that Tony sold me. We stopped at McDonald's that morning, went through the drive-through.

I had half of an Egg McMuffin and dumped the rest in the trash. I think about that other half, and my mouth salivates. How wasteful I was when I knew where my next meal was coming from.

I spend a couple of hours examining my room in the most minute detail. I look at all of the walls, examine all the baseboards. Under my bed, I find a large golden box, maybe five feet by three feet, and a foot and half tall. It is very heavy and pulling it out and pushing it back is almost too much to ask of my food-starved body.

I look into the bathroom attached to my room, a simple enough affair. A toilet, a clawfoot bathtub. All done in white, down to the floor tiles. I figure out that I have just enough chain to get to the toilet, but not enough to reach the bathtub.

I return to the bed when my curiosity is sated, sitting to think. At length, my jumbled thoughts turn to my captor again. I have so many questions about him.

Who is he? What does he want with me? Where did he bring me?

More importantly, will he let me go?

I lie down on the bed again, growing tired. My eyelids are heavy, so I close them.

When I wake again, he is sitting right beside me, his grey eyes piercing me. He looks down on me as if I were a spoiled lover and he the older beau that liked to indulge me.

I sit up, recoiling from him. As I stare at him distrustfully, his lips curve upward in the hint of a smile.

His expression doesn't reach the cool grey of his eyes though, and that fact gives me chills. He's younger than I thought, probably in his mid-thirties. And his body is well-muscled, honed. By what, I don't know.

Yet another mystery surrounding him.

"You're awake," he says, as simply as though I was a girlfriend and not a frigging captive.

I can feel his eyes on me, all over my skin. I try to breathe normally, but my heart is racing a million miles an hour. He looks thoughtful.

"You're prettier than I expected you to be." He leans closer, and I cringe. He places his hand on my bare thigh and chuckles at my scramble to get away.

He just grabs the chain that's connected to my wrist and loops it around his hand in a smooth motion. He gives it a yank, and I am pulled off balance. I tumble back on the bed.

"That's enough of that," he says mildly. He cocks his head. "I need a new name for you. Katherine Carolla is dead, so I need something feminine and... something small, like you."

"I'm not dead," I say, my voice shaking. I tug at the chain, but he doesn't even flinch.

"You aren't, no. But neither are you Katherine any

longer. I killed her when I bought her at the slave auction. Or didn't you notice?"

I make a face at the words slave auction. "So, you admit that you're the kind of man who hangs out at slave auctions, then?"

My words come out saltier than I meant them to, but he doesn't seem to take offense. He doesn't seem to hear me at all. He narrows his gaze on my face.

"Fiore," he says. "It means flower in Italian. I think that will be your new name, girl."

"My name is Katherine," I say, defiantly.

"You will soon learn how very wrong you are. You will soon learn a lot."

His grey gaze is heavy on my face, my breasts, the juncture of my thighs. It makes my skin crawl.

He's crazy, that much is evident. I need to get as much information from him as is possible, and then I can mull it over when I'm alone again.

"Where are we?" I say, switching topics.

He arches a brow. "Columbia. We are on my compound, alone except for the staff to keep things running smoothly. No one will help you." He pauses for a moment. "No one will come for you. You know that, right?"

I left my chin, tears pricking my eyes. "You don't know that."

He pulls on the chain, bringing me closer. "But I do, Fiore. I do know that. Your father sold you down the river, your brothers too. There is no one else, is there?"

I clamp down on my emotions, although I can't stop the tears from leaking down my cheeks.

"You're a monster," I tell him, tasting those same tears on my lips. "You don't know the first thing about me."

"No?" he says, something glinting in those deadly grey eyes.

He stands up, using the chain to force me over to the edge of the bed, kneeling. I can see the chain is cutting into his hand, but he seems unconcerned. He stands between my knees, holding the chain up high so that I can't sit on my heels.

He skims up my inner thigh with one hand, which makes me jump. His hand goes up, up... until he finds the nestle of curls just at the juncture of my thighs. His fingers probe my lower lips.

"No!" I say. When he slips a finger casually inside me, not the least bit concerned with how I feel, I scream in his face. "No! I said no! Stop!"

His finger inside my body is an absolute, unquestionable violation. I try to move, to close my knees against him, but he just lifts my handcuff painfully high.

The invasion of his rough touch is everything I have spent my entire life being told I should fear. So, I do fear it.

I fear *him*.

He leans in close, almost touching his face to mine. "You belong to me now, Fiore. I own you. I can do whatever I want to you, whenever I want it. And you'll do what I say, or I will kill you. It's as simple as that."

"Monster," I whisper, closing my eyes. As if that could shut him out. "What do you even want from me?"

He withdraws his finger from me and leans down until he's right next to my ear.

"Everything," he says, his breath tickling my ear and making goosebumps break out on my arms and legs. I feel a sudden sense of dread.

And then he releases my chain, walking out of the room

like he's got somewhere better to be. As if I'm not shaking and afraid. Like he didn't make me feel that way.

I am left staring as he slams the door shut, my mouth agape.

What.
The.
Hell.

5

KATHERINE

I wake to footsteps. I roll over, expecting him. Instead, it's two older men, carrying in a desk. They are dressed in a uniform of sorts, each wearing baggy grey pants, and a matching long sleeve shirt. I sit up, alarmed.

My stomach growls with hunger.

"Hello?" I ask, scrambling to the foot of the bed.

One of the men looks at me with something like pity in his wizened brown eyes, but the other speaks to him sternly in Spanish. He drops his eyes, chastised, and they move the desk to the corner by the window.

"You have to speak to me," I argue, darting out of bed. I step in front of one of them, blocking him from leaving.

Without meeting my eyes, he roughly shoves me aside, continuing on his way out of the room. I follow them as far as I can until my golden chain is pulled taut.

"Come back!" I call into the hallway. "Please! Hello?"

No response. Certainly not from Monster, which is what I've dubbed the man with the grey eyes and the timbre of voice that gives me chills.

Monster is the one who purchased me.

Swallowing, I push the thoughts of Monster away.

I look out into the hallway, which is done in the same dark wood floors. The walls that I can see are painted white instead of navy blue. There is a window at the very edge of my vision, but I can't make out anything else.

Then the men return again, this time carrying a beautiful gold, plush fainting couch. They put it against the wall by the door.

"I'm not supposed to be here," I tell the men as they move the couch. "It's a mistake. Please, do you have a phone? Or... could you call 911 for me? Please, I'm begging you here..."

The men act as though I'm not even present. They come in and out of the room, bringing a rack of blood red clothing, a chair, a pillow for the window seat. At last, the men bring in a silver serving tray of chicken, rice, an apple, and a big glass of water.

No fork, certainly no knife. But I fall upon the tray like the starving wretch that I am, almost not noticing that one of the men grasps my chain and unlocks the golden handcuff from my wrist.

I glare at him, rubbing my wrist, my mouth too full of food to complain. The food is so basic, but it tastes wonderful to me. I see the men leave the room, but I'm unable to leave the tray until I've literally licked the plate clean and eaten the apple down to the seeds and stem.

Because who knows when I might see food again? I don't, that's for sure. I've fallen off the edge of the world, down the rabbit hole, and landed here. Nothing makes sense in this strange place.

Truly, it's the first time that Alice in Wonderland has ever made complete sense to me.

After I lick my fingers clean, I am stunned to realize that the men left the door to the bedroom wide open. I no longer have the handcuff holding me back, so I move to the door.

Carefully, I poke my head out the doorway. I peer down the long white-walled hallway, taking in the window across from me, the closed doors to other rooms. I don't see anyone, which raises the question of whether or not I am supposed to have the run of the place.

I don't know. All I know is that I am barefoot and afraid... and that if my release is some kind of fluke, I don't care. All the news stories I've ever heard about girls that have been abducted and imprisoned ended with the girl taking advantage of a small mistake and walking away.

Oh, God... I'm one of those girls. Will my face be shown on the news? Will anyone even notice that I am missing?

Something tells me that they won't.

Panic rises in my chest, but I push it down. I don't have time for that right now... I'm definitely going to try to escape because this could be my only chance.

I touch the spot on my collarbone where he carved into my skin. It's healing now, really itchy. Pulling the little bandage off, I peer down at the wound, where it is pink and angry and puckered.

It's good to have a reminder of just what kind of stakes are involved here, I guess. That's the only silver lining I can find.

I leave the bedroom behind, padding quietly down the hall. I go first to the window on the other side of the hall, but when I look out, I find that the window just looks down upon an empty courtyard. I blink for a second at the building itself, done in white wood with elegant high windows carved here and there. It's very Spanish in its design, soaring and classic.

I look up to see the roof, which is finished in multicolored orange and red clay tiles. The house I'm in is actually breathtaking if I had the breath to give. As far as I can tell from counting the windows below, I'm on the third floor.

I give myself a shake, to stop from gawping at the view. Turning, my bare feet make me shiver as they tread the dark wood floor. As quickly as I can, I make my way through the maze of hallways, looking for a staircase.

I have to get down to the bottom floor. That's my best chance of escape.

As I roam the mansion — because there is absolutely no question that this is a mansion — I notice something pretty startling. Despite everything I've seen so far being spotless, there are no servants here, no one doing any work.

No one that I can beg for help, but also no one to hide from, either.

I find a staircase, at last, a small one made for servants, I presume. I fly down the stairs, ending up in a dark, cramped hall that is lined with brick. To my left, I hear the bustling sounds of women talking in Spanish and heavy machinery moving. Down the hall and to my right, there is a short flight of stairs. At the top of those stairs, there is a pair of doors thrown open wide, with sunlight pouring in from the outside.

And just like that, my plan of escape comes to life. Less of a plan and more of a mad dash, really. But I will take what I can get.

Looking both ways to make sure no one will see me, I sprint for the stairs. I make it up to the top, bursting outside. I'm surrounded by a little verdant yard, and then the hills immediately begin to rise, green, dramatic, and ivy-covered.

I run out to the first hill, eyeing the slope. It has to be at least forty-five degrees high. No one can climb that kind of a grade, not without climbing equipment. Frustrated, I bite my lip and decide to follow the bottom of the hill around the side of the house.

There must be another way out, somewhere.

"I wouldn't do that," says a deep male voice. I turn around and find several men standing in the doorway I just escaped from. At a glance, the men appear that they are probably from South America, and they are dressed like they are in the military. They are all well-muscled and scowling, all wearing tactical vests and the same red bandanas. Two of them hold rifles, their ease with the weapons speaking volumes.

While I stand frozen in my tracks, the man who spoke steps forward. "Our master doesn't want you to be lost. We will track you down if need be. Come back inside."

The two men with rifles swing the guns in my direction, and I blanch. "No, you don't understand..."

"You don't need to plead your case to me. The master has spoken." He crosses his arms impatiently.

The master? My head is full of a thousand thoughts suddenly, trying to figure out who that could be.

Then it becomes clear who he's talking about. The tall Mediterranean-looking man, with the grey eyes that pierce right through me. The man I've been calling Monster in my head.

I want to run. I want to scream. But somehow, I don't think that either action will do much to help me. Not with the squadron of men staring me down.

Then something occurs to me.

"You're here to guard me?" I ask, cocking my head.

The man looks at me for a long moment, as if trying to

decide whether to answer me or not. Finally, he just nods. "Yes."

"Your master would probably be angry with you if anything happened to me," I say, knowing that it's a gamble. "I'm betting that you wouldn't like what happens to you if he was to get angry."

I catch the moment of shock in his eyes before he glowers at me again. "We have our instructions. Just because we can't kill you doesn't mean we won't hurt you."

Frustrated, I lash out. "I think you won't do anything if I run."

Without a moment's hesitation, he says, "I will beat you."

I narrow my eyes. "I don't think you're telling the truth."

"Try me" he threatens.

I stare at him, my pulse picking up. Then I turn and sprint away to the very bottom of the hill, following it as it meanders around the mansion.

I don't get very far, not that I really expected to. In a flash, the men are after me, and it's not long before their long legs catch up with my shorter ones. The man who was talking catches me around the waist with a kind of ease that speaks of honed skills.

He scoops me up in a squirming, indignant ball and carries me back to the house.

"No! Let me go! I don't belong here!" I protest.

As soon as he reaches the brick stairwell, the second that he can, he allows me to tumble to the floor. I look up at him, wondering if the exercise even managed to wind him. I am certainly a mess, breathing hard, and now my knees are skinned on top of it all.

"Don't do that," he says, folding his arms across his chest. "Don't make us chase you around. Stay in the house."

I shove my long blonde hair out of my face, furious. "You don't tell me what to do."

He gives me a look. "That's right, I don't. The master tells you what to do. I just follow his orders. And you will too if you know what is good for you."

Standing up, I storm into the house. I don't see them following me, but I can feel their eyes on me anyway. There is no doubt that they will trail me from a distance, none at all.

I steam as I head back up the staircase, retracing my steps. I need to think, to formulate a plan for my escape. I don't know where Monster is, but my need to get away from here, from him, is nearly overwhelming.

I need time to plot and to cool my racing heart.

6

KATHERINE

I'm on the auction platform, staring out at an audience full of men in black face masks. Everything is fuzzy around the edges, dreamlike. Moving in slower motion than normal.

I'm led to the right spot on the stage by a man with work-roughened hands, a man with a black face mask like the rest of the men looking at me.

Judging me.

Finding me wanting.

Thinking I'm lacking in one way or another.

They ogle me, their eyes greedy. As if they are trying to tell whether I am even worthwhile or not.

The auctioneer is calling something out, but I'm too fixed by my own private congregants to hear him. I feel their eyes on me, feel them probing. There is a current in this room; an energy that makes me jumpy.

I remind myself yet again that I'm not crazy; half the men in this room want to fuck me, the other half want something much darker from me.

My blood rushes through my ears, nearly deafening me.

I make eye contact with one man, one man who stands in the back, yet stands out from the rest of the crowd. I don't know why he catches my attention, but the look in his eyes...

His glittering and dark eyes...

It's madness perhaps, or mania. The look of someone who is very close to getting what he wants, and now he's just impatiently waiting until it drops into his lap.

I drop my gaze, looking away with a shudder of fear. The drugs dull every sensation, but it seems as though that man stares at me so sharply that I can actually feel the blades sliding into my skin. It's a very intense impression, in this blurry-edged world.

While I am staring at the ground, there is a commotion. Then a gunshot, its sound so loud that I'm absolutely sure that my heart is going to gallop out of my chest. I hunch down, and there is some shouting among the men.

It's only when I taste the blood, that I realize I have bitten my tongue. I glance up, frightened and shaking. The guard in his black mask begins to pull me away, dragging me when I don't cooperate.

I am pulled back toward the back area, and then I change hands, yet another huge man in a black mask taking charge of me. He bundles me over toward the warehouse's exit, toward that same man that I made eye contact with before.

I can almost smell the excitement pouring from the manic man. He looks me up and down, his lips lifting in the ghost of a smile.

"I am your master now," he says. His accent is thick, but his English perfect.

Then he pulls up a switchblade, and my heart begins to race.

No. Please God, no.

I think the words, but nothing comes out of my mouth. Instead, the huge man grabs me from behind, holding my arms back. My eyes widen as the other man steps up to me, smiling, and slices the flesh of my collarbone.

I shriek as the knife carves into my skin, blood rushing up to the surface and covering the knife.

Then I open my eyes, my mouth forming a silent scream. It takes a few heart-pounding seconds for me to come awake fully, lying on my back in another room entirely. I stare at the royal blue ceiling, my heart racing, sweat cooling on my skin.

Where am I?

What am I doing here?

Where is my family?

Then it all comes rushing back to me at once. It wasn't a dream, it was a memory.

I'm somewhere in South America.

I'm here because Monster bid for me, shot someone, and emerged victoriously.

And I'll never see any of my family again because they sold me.

They *sold* me.

My eyes fill with tears, and I turn onto my side, curling up in a ball of my own misery. A sob catches in my chest. For a minute I just let the tears come, breaking down and crying.

"What are you crying for, Fiore?"

I roll over in the bed, furiously wiping at my face. Monster stands in the doorway, filling up the space with his big frame, his head cocked. My first inclination is to ignore him, but right on the heels of that is another instinct.

Talk to him. At least he speaks to you, unlike everyone else in this house.

Well, everyone but the guard.

I sit up, sniffling and wary. I feel very vulnerable like this, sitting in the middle of the bed, with him looking at me with a patient expression. I'm willing to bet that patience only lasts for a moment or two.

I lift my chin. "That's not my name."

He has the temerity to look disappointed. "I told you, Katherine Carolla is dead. I killed her. Strangled her to death with my bare hands."

His accent is not quite Middle Eastern, and not quite Italian. I struggle to put a name to it. Yet another mystery.

I wrap my arms around myself, a small comfort. "I don't care what you say."

"No?" he asks, stepping into the room. He snaps his fingers, and a young woman comes in with a silver serving tray. She sets it down on the bed, then scurries back out of the room.

An appetizing aroma escapes from the plates on the tray, and my stomach growls. I clamber across the bed, reaching for the tray, but Monster clicks his tongue.

"Tsk, tsk. That food is for Fiore," he says, sauntering over to my bed. He pulls the tray a few inches away from me.

I look at the tray, then look up at him. He's clearly offering a trade of some kind. "What do you want?"

He gives me a long look. "I want you to call yourself by your new name. It's as simple as that."

"Fiore?" I ask, frowning. "You just want me to call myself that?"

He nods slowly, a little pucker forming in his brow. "It really is asking very little of you... for now."

I grimace. "Fine."

His eyebrows lift. "Fine? Fine what?"

I heave a sigh like he has asked me to do something challenging. "Fine, I'm Fiore. Whatever you want me to call myself."

I reach for the tray, but he pulls it back. "No. Say it as if you mean it."

"What do you mean, as I mean it?" I ask, looking up at him.

He waves a hand. "Convince me that you mean your name is Fiore. Then you can eat. I would hurry because the food is getting cold."

My mouth pulls to the side as my stomach rumbles again. I glance at the tray of food, swallowing. He's right about this one thing... he's really not asking much.

I push aside the rebellious thoughts, the ones about how I wouldn't even be here if it weren't for him. Food is more important than any thoughts of insurgency I might have.

I raise my chin and meet his eyes. "I am Fiore."

He looks unsatisfied. "And what do you want, right now?"

I pull a face. "What do I want? I want to leave."

He sits back with a sigh. "Don't be tiresome. Do you want the food or no?"

"I do." I try not to sound reticent, but even to my ears, it sounds pouty.

"All together," he coaches. "Who are you and what do you want?"

I narrow my gaze at him. "I'm Fiore. I want this food."

"This food?" he asks, uncovering one of the plates to reveal a beef stew. "You want what I brought here for you?"

"Yes!" I snap, glaring at him.

"All right," he says, pushing the tray towards me. "Go ahead."

There is no silverware on the tray, so I just go at the stew with my hands, trying to shovel as much into my mouth at once as possible. It's still warm on my fingers, the salty goodness of beef and vegetables coating my tongue and throat.

Monster watches me eat with a trace of amusement.

"You're disgusting," he says casually, as though I would choose this on my own.

I don't look at him. I focus on the food, on how amazing it tastes, at how good it feels to be filling my body with sustenance.

I see his hand dart out and remove the cover from another smaller plate, revealing a little dab of what looks like rice pudding. I glance at him for a second, unsure.

Why would he bring me dessert?

Then again, it is pointless to wonder why. Why does he keep me prisoner? Why did he bring me to Colombia? What does he plan to do with me?

These are all good questions, but ones without an answer.

While I finish the last bit of beef stew, he folds his hands in his lap, almost looking prayerful.

"You tried to escape yesterday in my absence," he says mildly.

My eyes meet his, finding him strangely calm. I don't say anything, I just lick my fingers clean. I look at the rice pudding, still hungry.

"You won't do that again," he says. "Or you will face severe consequences. Do you understand?"

He toys with the plate that the rice pudding is on.

There is an awkward moment between us until he speaks again.

"You can have the dessert if you say that you understand." His face is blank, emotionless.

I bite my lip for a second, then nod. "I understand."

He moves his hand and I immediately scoop up a bit of the gooey, sticky pudding. I put my fingers into my mouth, involuntarily moaning a little bit as the sweet pudding hits my taste buds. I close my eyes, taking a moment to savor it.

I swear, I've never tasted anything so good in my whole entire life.

"Your hair is dyed," he notes.

I open my eyes to find him staring at me, at my hair. It's creepy like he's cataloging me for a library collection or something. I swallow but don't say anything back. He doesn't really expect me to say anything, I assume.

"I don't like anything fake or false on you. You don't need pretense," he says thoughtfully. "I'll send someone to correct your hair."

"What?" I say, my mouth still full of pudding.

He looks disgusted. "You'll swallow your food before speaking."

My cheeks heat with shame. "You have an awful lot of bullshit rules."

He stands up, sweeping the entire heavy silver food tray off the bed with one hand. He glowers at me. "You should think twice before you speak, girl."

"My name is Katherine!" I pop off, without really thinking.

The next thing I know, he's pulling me off of the bed, grabbing me around the waist so hard that I hear something snap. I cry out, the sound strangled, and he grips my throat. My eyes widen as he gets right up close to my face, close enough that I can feel the heat of his breath on my chin.

"Watch what you say to me," he threatens, squeezing his hand that is on my throat. "I will fucking kill you, I swear to God."

My hands fly up to try to pull his hand away, but he tosses me to the floor like a rag doll and storms out of the room. Only then do the tears come again, the shock wearing a little thin.

I made a mistake with him. My mistake was treating him as though we were playing by society's rules, rules that say he would never be allowed to touch me. Never be allowed to hit a woman.

I pull my knees up to my chest, wincing at the pain in my side, and wipe tears from my eyes. He might've actually broken a rib.

I don't know what I will do with him in the future, but I know one thing.

He is not to be trifled with.

7
KATHERINE

For the next few days, I'm mostly on my own. Meal trays arrive once a day, left outside my door with cheese, bread, and an apple. I leave the trays out in the hall when I'm done, and they're ferried away again.

One of the older women comes into my room with a box of hair dye. After trying to talk to talk to her, and again being unsuccessful, I just let her dye my long blonde tresses. When she's done, the color is pretty close to my natural color... as if I never even had highlights put in.

It's like Monster is erasing little pieces of my past, bit by bit. I find that more depressing than anything.

For the rest of my time, I continue to explore my room. I luxuriate in taking a bath, washing a lot of the filth that I've been building up away. I soak in the bathtub until the water begins to turn my hands pruny and the bath turns cool.

I wander out of the bath to find the blood red dresses hanging on their rack, waiting for me to don them. Since there are no towels in my bathroom, I dry my hair on one of the dresses and my body on another.

I slip the sheath over my head, frustrated still at the lack of undergarments. Even a pair of basic cotton granny panties would be welcome at this point. There is no mirror in my room, just like there are no shoes for my feet or sheets for my bed.

Everything is just inconvenient, adding to the baseline fact that I'm in a strange place with strange people.

I refuse to let myself use the word *kidnapped*. Swallowing the lump in my throat, I try not to imagine how my life would be if I had run away from my home in New Orleans when Tony first warned me.

Much better not to think about it and keep exploring instead.

When I've explored the bedroom in minute detail, I turn my attention to memorizing the house and grounds. First the top two floors, where empty rooms echo strangely and there are white sheets covering the odd pieces of furniture scattered about like ghosts.

As I explore, I think about who I should try to contact. Not my family, obviously, even though I miss them a lot at times. I trusted them completely when in hindsight they were always a little... weird and gross.

I can never go back to them, that much is clear.

So, that leaves other people, like the police. Would the police in Columbia care about a kidnapped girl, though? Especially a foreigner? My inclination is no, they wouldn't.

But that doesn't rule out all types of police. The FBI or CIA could potentially be good contacts. Or maybe someone on the street here? A priest, a young woman weaving baskets, a farmer.

They would be good because they would have the ability to alert the proper authorities. I mull over all the possibilities as I go from room to room, not finding anything of great interest.

There are a few locked rooms at the end of one hall, but I can't hear anything when I put my ear to their doors. Maybe these rooms are where Monster stays?

So, I explore the bottom floor, including the kitchen and the laundry, both filled with the same obstinate and unhearing serving women. I snoop through both rooms without hesitation or shame. I refuse to cower or hide from them anymore. They must have some inkling of my situation, they are just paid very well to close themselves off to me.

I save the mansion's grounds for last, everything inside the wall. The miniature orchard below my window, the grand driveway ending in the most secure gates I've ever seen. The wall is quaint stone, but the gates are high, tall steel monstrosities surrounded by razor wire.

I have the same grim-faced security detail most of the time, including the man that grabbed me and dumped me back inside. They trail me silently wherever I go.

Something strikes me as I lead them through the cherry orchard. There is a sort of power in my position because they don't say anything or do anything as long as I am not trying to escape. They're the same as the women in that way, not benevolent by any means, but not actively out to hurt me.

When I discover the stables on the far edge of the mansion's grounds, I'm elated. Back in New Orleans, I rode horses religiously for years, keeping several horses in a prestigious stable... until we ran out of money, that is. My heart swells with a curious sense of home the second I lay eyes on the building.

But when I head toward the stable, that same younger guard that I tussled with before speaks up. "No. You aren't allowed to go in there."

I turn, shading my eyes and glancing back at him. "Why not?"

He just shrugs, as if he could not care less. I frown at him, but I don't push things today. My plan to learn every inch of the grounds doesn't hinge on exploring that. I'm satisfied just knowing that it's there.

Eventually, when I know the whole place better, I will hatch some kind of escape plan. But for now, I just walk away from the stables, staring at the guards.

"What does he pay you?" I ask the younger one, cocking my head. "To keep kidnapped girls on this property. I hope that you're making a lot of money."

He doesn't react. "None of your business."

I continue as though he hadn't spoken. "I figure between you guys and the women inside, he's gotta be paying... what, a million dollars a year? Two million? That's a pretty decent rate of pay, I'll admit. I mean, it's not worth the jail time you face, but..."

His eyes narrow a little and he shifts his stance. "You talk too much."

I look at him, considering. Just how far has Monster told them to take guarding me? What would Monster do if I acted a little *too* interested in one of the guards? How would Monster react to me being attracted to one of them?

I decide to try it. What's the worst that will happen? I've already been kidnapped and sold at a slave auction. It can't get much worse than that.

That little bit of knowledge makes my lips lift just a little. I look at the young guard.

"What's your name?" I ask casually.

He lifts a brow, folding his arms across his thick chest. "You can call me Sin."

I purse my lips and try to put on a seductive pout. "That's all I get? Just Sin?"

Sin's eyes narrow. "That's enough for you."

"What if it isn't, though?" I say. I saunter toward him or try to saunter at least. "What if I want more?"

He scowls. "You're talking too much again."

"Oh, yeah? Maybe I should do something else, then. But what?" I get a yard away from him, closing the gap between us slowly. I watch him go on high alert. It's like two puzzle pieces click together in his head, and I can see it on his face.

Sin reaches for the gun at his hip but doesn't pull it. "Stop that."

I play dumb and innocent. "Stop what? I'm not doing anything."

Sin looks around and licks his lips. "Are you fucking crazy? Ar— our master — will kill us both if he sees you doing this."

I look left and right, then stage whisper to him. "He's not here to see anything."

Then he gives away a secret by looking at the house, *hard*. "He is everywhere. You don't understand."

Does that mean that there are cameras mounted everywhere? Or does Sin refer to the maid staff?

I shrug, turning myself to avoid him entirely. I start to head back inside the house. "Your loss."

I can feel Sin's eyes like daggers in my back, but I don't turn around. I do sashay my hips a bit as I walk away, to make him stare at my ass as I leave. He doesn't say anything, just stays put outside.

I spend the rest of my day daydreaming of escape. I think of ways that I could just slip past the guards and walk into the Colombian forest that surrounds the house, somehow unnoticed.

I fall asleep at dark, my dreams carrying me away.

When I open my eyes again, I blink as the overhead lights that I didn't even realize were in my room are turned on with a snap. I sit up groggily, and then I realize that Monster has returned from wherever he had gone.

I realize this because he is charging toward me, his grey eyes sparking with fury. His long legs eat up the space between the doorway and the bed. Before I can really even react, he grabs me hard by the shoulders, lifting me. He gives me several sharp shakes, bringing his face down close to mine.

"You are a fool," he hisses, digging his fingers into my flesh. This close, I can see he hasn't shaved today, can smell a deep note of dusky sandalwood in the air.

My first sleepy thought is that he is almost breathtakingly handsome, his features carved from some otherworldly stone.

I'm sort of bewildered. By his sudden presence, but also by what time it is. A glance out the big bay window proves that it is still dark outside.

"I—" I start, but he shakes me again.

"No, you don't talk," he sneers, breathing raggedly. "You think you can just talk to my bodyguards? Well, I think it's time you learned about the box."

The box? I scramble to put together what he's saying. *What box?*

He shoves me back onto the bed, leaning down to drag out the golden box from underneath my bed. My mouth opens a little as he pries off the heavy lid, revealing crushed velvet inside.

Surely, he doesn't mean to put me in there?

But he grabs my ankles and drags me off the bed. An involuntary scream leaves my lips.

"No!" I say. "What are you doing?"

He's much too strong for me to do anything but struggle as he wrestles me into the tiny box. I scream as he manages to hold me down long enough to get the lid on, sealing me inside the tomblike box.

It's dark in here, and I can barely move. I am instantly claustrophobic, struggling to breathe.

"No! Let me out! Monster, please!" I scream, banging my fists on the lid. "Please! I can't breathe!"

I can barely hear him moving around over the thump, thump, thump of my own heart. I try again to move the lid, using my whole body to shove up at it, but it's no use. All I can think as I start to sob is that I'm in my own coffin. I imagine my mother probably felt just like this when she was dying in that old cabin, all alone.

I claw at the lid, begging and crying. "Please! Monster, I know that you're out there! Please, you don't understand..."

I hear him shift his stance, but nothing more than that. He's probably trying to figure out how he ended up buying someone so crazy. I think these things as I scratch at the lid, tearing my own nail beds ragged.

"Help me," I blubber, feeling overwhelmed. My throat feels scratchy and hoarse from yelling. "Oh, God, please help..."

I am highly aware of every breath that I take, of every single inch of my body, of the couple of inches between me and the lid. I close my eyes, shutting out the darkness, and try to calm my tears.

There are several more minutes of tear-stained shuddered breaths, and then I finally fall silent. My eyes and fists are clenched, futile in this moment.

I'm dead. I didn't survive the kidnapping, and this is hell.

Strangely, that thought comforts me. My breathing grows deeper and easier, my mind quiets a bit. As long as I don't think about where I am, I can sort of... just be. Like my mind is floating somewhere, jellyfish-like, far away from here.

I picture that and enter some in-between state, not quite awake, not quite asleep. Not peaceful, but just... not here. It's kind of nice.

Monster lifts the lid suddenly, plunging me back into reality. His expression is mainly curious; whatever anger he felt has faded away.

"What did you call me?" he asks, peering down at me.

"Monster," I whisper, meeting his eyes. "I call you what you are."

He appears amused. "That's exactly what I am, Fiore."

Then he turns and walks out of my bedroom, cool, calm, and collected. I'm left to drag myself out of the box and shove it back underneath the bed, shaking with endorphins.

I'm so confused about what just happened, I don't even know what to do.

Who smiles and agrees that they should be called Monster?

8

ARSEN

I dream of my brothers Damen and Dryas that night. I dream that I am young again, maybe ten summers. Father has disappeared, and my mother has taken to her bed with her pipe, smoking a little so that she won't wake up shaking at night.

The three of us sit on a bridge, underneath the full summer moon, staring down at the water. Silence weighs us down as the distant blare of a ship's horn sounds in the eerie night.

We've been shooed out of the house so that our mother can sleep peacefully. After a little pickpocketing down by the docks, which will pay for a chunk of bread each, we've settled here to sit and wait.

Damen scratches his head furiously. I eye him, thinking that it's been a while since we had our heads shaved. We don't want to catch lice again, or any number of the other things that live in hair.

Since I'm older than Damen by a year, it's my job to make sure that he's vermin free.

I chew the last bit of my bread, noticing that Dryas

hasn't even touched his yet. His dark head is lowered, his eyes focused on the water.

Just nine months older than I am, he always has been the introspective one of the three of us. He heaves a sigh, thinking heavy thoughts.

"What?" I ask, leaning back on my elbows. "You thinking about how the rent is going to be paid again? I told you, we have ten days to figure it out."

Dryas slowly shakes his head. "No."

"Then what?" I ask, my gaze sliding over to Damen again. Damen seems oblivious to our talk, in his own world entirely. I suspect that he hears more than he lets on, though.

"What if she dies?" Dryas says, sounding concerned.

"Who? Mother?" I ask my face pinching with concentration.

"Yeah. That's what I heard Pallis say when some guys came looking for lodging. That he expects our apartment to be available soon enough because Mother is sick."

I'm a little taken aback. "Sick? How is she sick? She doesn't have a cough..."

He nods, still staring down at the water. "Pallis said that she slept with the wrong kind of men. She's got the same disease that so many street women die from."

He screws his face up, glancing at the full moon. I consider the fact that Mother could be dying, and I feel surprisingly little. Really, she started to slip away when Father left, when she took up the pipe that makes her sleep.

For the last three years, my brothers and I have been mostly on our own. We have been paying the rent and feeding Mother. Without her, I honestly feel like we'll be better off.

I don't tell Dryas that, though. Instead, I change the subject.

"Tell me again what the mafia man told you?" I say.

Dryas lights up a little. "He says that we're almost old enough to join the mafia. Probably a year for me, and two for you. Once we do that, we'll be set. We just have to go through their ritual to join..."

"I wonder what that could be?" I say, excitedly.

Dryas looks at me, his face morphing, growing older. It's still just the three of us, but now I'm eighteen, legally a man. We're holed up in some second-story apartment, with Damen peering out of the blinds to see our targets as soon as they arrive in the alley below. He squints and shuffles his deck of tarot cards, silent as usual.

If I didn't know any better, I would think that Damen was softer than Dryas and me. In reality though, I know that Damen is not cool and calculating. He actually kills for *fun*. The youngest of the three of us ended up being a bloody psychopath.

I can't blame him after what he has seen.

"I think we would be stupid not to go to London," Dryas says. He lights a cigarette and takes a puff, considering. He shrugs. "If the Cypriot will have us, I don't see any downside."

"We'll be leaving everything we've ever known. We're probably going to die within a week of stepping foot on foreign soil," I say, glancing away.

Dryas chuckles. "Oh? Speak for yourself. I'm immortal."

I slide him a glance. "I'm serious, Dryas."

"So am I! Besides, you're just worried about leaving that whore you've been fucking. There is a whole world of whores, little brother."

I scowl. He's not wrong. I am a little concerned about leaving the luscious piece of ass I've been losing myself in lately. But more than that, I am worried about Dryas's ambitions.

The man thinks that he will take over the Cypriot mafia family, and he thinks that this is the right step to do it. He just doesn't say it out loud.

What he doesn't realize is that I've already talked to the higher-ups about London. I'm definitely going, with or without Dryas and Damen.

He's not the only one with ambitions.

I look over at Damen. "Any sign of Fiore?"

Damen looks confused. "Shouldn't you be more worried about Anna? She did die because of you, after all--"

And then I'm suddenly yanked backward, out of the dream.

That doesn't seem right, asking about Fiore. That's not what I said, is it? And that part about Anna... my timeline is all screwed up, somehow.

I shift in my sleep, waking gradually. I open my eyes in the pitch black, which is how I prefer my bedroom. Climbing out of bed, I walk naked to my window, flinging the curtains wide. I wince at the bright sunlight that pours in, illuminating my body.

I stand there for a moment, trying to process the dream I just had. For the most part, it was accurate... except for that bit at the very end. I never mentioned her back then; hell, I didn't even conceive of such a person existing in my world until a few months ago.

Just like I hadn't ever seen the bloody head of a woman

I was fucking arrive on my doorstep. I guess those were simpler times...

What I get out of this morning's addition to my dream is that the girl has gotten under my skin, has wormed her way into my dreams. For such a skinny little girl, Fiore takes up too much space in my brain.

She occupies my thoughts more than I planned. Aside from reminding me of Anna, she is generally quite pleasant to look at. Actually, she's extremely pretty, with creamy pale skin and those wide blue eyes. Her mouth is bewitching, pouty, and plump.

The things I would like to do that mouth make me lie awake at night.

I picture her when I'm traveling, wondering what she might be up to. Imagining the pleasure I will have once I've broken her, body and spirit, and made her crave death.

Staring out the window, I get hard as I imagine her on her knees, a sweet little virgin begging me not to violate her. Then I wonder if maybe she will surprise me and beg for me to fuck her instead, to punish her with my cock.

Either way, it will be pleasant for me. Closing my eyes, I fist my cock, stroking it lazily as I think about her moans of pleasure blended with pain. I imagine her begging me for my cock, her soft pink lips closing around the very tip.

I groan when I think that I will be the only one to ruin her perfect innocence, to steal her virginity. And she's going to plead for me to do it... I never take anything from women that isn't mine by right.

No, Fiore will beg for my cock before I punish her by plunging the entire length into her. I have a massive cock, so I expect it to *hurt* when I finally take her virginity.

The thought makes my lips curve upwards in the hint of a smile.

I am not a nice man. I'm no one's idea of the guy you take home to meet your parents. I will never be the super sweet boyfriend that listens to your worries and kisses away your fears.

I'm something else entirely. I am an assassin, a cold-hearted businessman, and the shadow in the alley when you're walking home. I am dangerous, and I have no problems with that.

People are afraid of me, including the whores that I sleep with. I have absolutely no compunction about acting on my basest impulses, and no reason to stop myself.

So, I think about ruining her, shredding everything that is decent and moral in Fiore's life. And it spurs me on, makes me harder.

When someone knocks on my door, I don't pause. I just stay standing by the window, lost in my own world. The second knock is just background noise.

When Damen's voice cuts through my pleasure, I am taken aback.

"Arsen, your little slave girl is trying to escape," my brother calls. "It would be funny if it weren't so pathetic."

Grabbing my black silk robe and flinging it on, I pad to the door and rip it open.

"What the fuck are you doing here?" I demand.

Damen shrugs. "I came to see you, brother. Besides, I'm not the one that you should be worried about. Your multi-million-dollar purchase is in the kitchens, scrounging for food she can take when she escapes. She left this just lying around in her room."

He holds up a piece of paper, which I snatch from his fingertips. It's a list written in a feminine hand, detailing all the things that she should gather and pack for her attempt at escape. I read it briefly, then crumple it in my hand.

I fix Damen with a steely glare, not trusting him for one fucking second. He has done nothing but make my life harder since I took over the New Orleans territory, and now he just shows up here?

Unlikely.

I also have a bone to pick with him getting much too close to Fiore, but that's for another time. I shoulder past him and head down the front stairs toward the kitchen, my fury reaching into my ice-cold heart and filling it with an unquenchable fire.

9

KATHERINE

I sneak up the back staircase, carrying a tea towel full of food that won't spoil easily. It's the third bullet point in the list that I scribbled down after I found the purses and light jackets of the women who work in the kitchen.

Food that won't turn and something to carry it in.

While the women were upstairs cleaning, I snuck into the little closet that I've seen them coming and going from and found all their stuff.

I didn't even think twice about robbing them. Screw those women for getting paid enough to overlook a captive amongst them. I didn't wince as I took a little bit of money, several pens, a penknife, and a pad of paper.

I stayed up late, thinking and plotting. Writing on my newfound stash of paper.

Today, I went back to the basement floor and waited until they were occupied upstairs. Then I took some food from the pantry, a little of this and a little that. Not so much that it will be noticed, just a few days' worth of bread and cheese and a couple of apples.

Then I grabbed the first thing I saw to contain it in, a freshly cleaned tea towel, and I slipped out of the kitchens. It's as easy as that.

Now, with my heart pounding, I race upstairs as fast as my legs will carry me. When I get close to my room though, I hear Monster storming down the hall. How did he know about it so quickly? I only just went downstairs!

As I round the corner and duck into my room, I look for somewhere to hide my tea towel. Frantic, I dump it all in the bathtub and partially close the bathroom door behind me.

I don't even make it to the bed before Monster marches in, looking upset. Maybe upset is too nice a word for it... he looks murderous. My heart begins to pound in my chest.

"What the fuck do you think you're doing?" he snarls, grabbing me by the arm. He gives me a sharp shake that's hard enough to make my head snap backward. He's so much bigger than me, he could easily hurt me or kill me with very little effort.

I swallow the huge lump that forms in my throat.

"Nothing!" I insist, acting as if I don't know why he's upset.

"Liar," he insists, shaking me again. "Don't bother trying to spin your web, you stupid girl. My brother found your little note."

I feel myself go pale. "I... It was—"

He cuts me off. "No, no more."

Monster thrusts me face first onto the bed, then he begins pulling out The Box. At the first flash of gold, my chest seizes up. I remember all too well what it felt like to be sealed inside.

Words pour out of my mouth, promising him absolutely anything to avoid The Box.

"No! Monster, please!" I plead, dread filling my heart as I look at The Box with wide, frightened eyes. "I swear, I'll do anything! Anything but that!"

He rips the lid off of The Box, pausing for a beat. His grey eyes are alight with fury.

"Get undressed," he says, his words angry.

I don't ask questions. I just slip my dress over my head, throwing it aside onto the bed. I shiver convulsively, feeling more naked than I've ever felt before. He takes a moment to look at me, his eyes probing me in all kinds of places that I desperately wish were still private.

"Stop moving," he commands, leaving The Box on the floor and rising to his feet.

I hold my breath and force myself to stay still. I notice that instead of his usual getup of dark slacks and a dark button-up, he's wearing a black silk robe. As if I interrupted his dressing routine or got him out of bed suddenly, somehow.

I watch him prowl around the bed, my body flushing hotly under his gaze. If I could go back in time, I would have put some conditions on my offer to do anything he asked. *Anything* is too much, too permissive.

I desperately watch his face, searching for a clue about what he is thinking. I don't want The Box, but neither am I going to give up my virginity to him willingly. Surely, he won't ask that much of me, not for such a small infraction.

I tremble as I feel his gaze as it lingers on my breasts, my pussy, the round globes of my ass.

"You want to avoid the box?" he asks, his hungry eyes coming up to rest on my face.

I swallow again, licking my lips. My answer comes out in a whisper. "Yes."

He cocks his head, a cruel smirk playing across his lips. "I want to watch you touch yourself."

My heart drops to my stomach. I don't think I heard him correctly. "Wh— what?"

"You heard me." He folds his muscular arms across his chest. "Lie down and spread your legs. Give me a show. Make me more interested in watching you masturbate than hearing you scream inside the box."

I bite my lip, blushing to my roots. "But... why?"

He glares at me. "Because, little girl, you interrupted me this morning. Just when I had my cock nice and hard. If you want to avoid the box, you'd better fix that right away."

I drop my eyes, unable to meet his gaze. The fact that he just admitted to masturbating is one thing, but the fact that he wants me to do it? Here, now? In front of him, while he presumably gets pleasure from it?

That makes me die a little bit inside.

I glance at The Box, shuddering because I remember being locked inside there, with no light, thinking I was going to choke to death.

I'm stuck between two awful choices, but it's pretty clear that one option makes me irrationally afraid. The other just skeeves me out.

I have to do what he asks. I glance up at him, and he can see my answer written in my eyes. A fleeting smile passes over his face.

"Good decision," he says, biting off the words like they're chewy. He waves a hand. "Get going. I want to see *everything*."

Trembling and blushing like mad, I lie down, my heartbeat as wild as a rabbit's. I can't believe I'm about to do this; I don't even touch myself very often at home. I never know who is listening, or who might burst into my room.

"You're already doing it wrong," Monster says, arching a brow. He motions for me to come closer. "Come down here to the end of the bed so I can see you."

I scoot down to the end of the bed, shaking and blushing. I sit at the end, lying back.

"You're not selling this as a good alternative to being in the box," he says, his tone bored. "Are you going to make me change my mind and rescind my offer?"

I shake my head, feeling tears of shame prick the corners of my eyes. I run my hands down my torso, feeling my breasts, my hipbones. I pet my thighs and my mons, stroking them over and over in a slow rhythm.

"Spread your thighs apart," Monster urges impatiently.

I follow his orders, finding myself perversely glad that he is telling me what to do. This is a situation of his creation, so I shouldn't feel anything but angry at him. But as I part my thighs and widen my knees on the end of the bed, I can't find that emotion amongst the swirl of feelings inside my head.

I slip two fingers down the crease of my pussy, trying not to watch him but failing. His eyes are fixated on my every movement as he begins to untie the sash of his robe. He's completely naked underneath, his musculature intense and beautiful.

And his... his penis...

I haven't known that many, certainly never any so close as the few feet that separate me from him. But hold crap, I don't recall ever seeing one so *big*. It's... it's monstrous.

How fitting, that Monster should be so well-endowed. He can barely fit his fist around his... member. He strokes it roughly, which makes me wonder if that's what... how... he likes sex.

My face flames as I have the thought. I need to focus on what I am doing instead of him.

Monster's gaze flits to my face. "Wet your fingers with your tongue."

I shake like a leaf as I bring my fingers up to my mouth, closing my lips around them. My saliva coats the tips of my fingers, and I put my fingers back down between my legs.

I close my eyes and turn my head away from him as I gently probe my clit and my lower lips. My heart pounds in my ears as I circle my clit ever so gently, then dip a finger into my entrance.

To my surprise, I'm not bone dry. No, it seems that somehow a little... stimulation goes a long way toward getting me nice and juicy.

I'm ashamed of myself, but I try not to think of that right now. Instead, I focus on my clit, using the pads off two fingers to circle it slowly.

"Look at me," Monster says, his voice little more than a rumble in his chest.

I open my eyes, biting my lip, and look up at him. He leans over me, not touching but still much too close, working his fist up and down his dick. He licks his lips, his excitement palpable.

"Tell me how it feels," he rumbles. "Or make sounds. Do something for me."

If I have to describe anything out loud, I am sure that I will literally die. So instead, I lean my head back, looking at the dark blue ceiling, and make breathy sounds. At first, they're kind of forced, but then... then they're not.

I let out a moan as I begin to move my fingers a little faster. I shouldn't be turned on by this, but the knowledge that this is off limits — that this is totally taboo — only spurs me on.

My hips start to jerk rhythmically, in time with some mysterious drumbeat that only I can hear.

"Fuck," Monster growls, his voice urgent. "Sit up, Fiore. Sit up!"

Confused, I prop myself up on one elbow. He's flushed and breathing hard, jackhammering his dick directly at me. I'm so flustered, I don't know what I'm supposed to do.

He pins me with his eyes, that perfect grey gaze seeming to go right through me. I turn my head a little, but I never break his gaze.

He groans and stiffens, then unleashes several long squirts of hot white stickiness onto my bare breasts and my upper stomach. I'm so surprised, all I can do is sit there like a slack-jawed idiot, blinking up at him.

He strokes his penis slower and slower, eventually stopping. He draws his robe closed over himself, tying the sash. He surveys me with a critical eye.

"Clean yourself up." He sounds distasteful. "Quickly, before I have the maids come in to fix the mess you made with their things."

Monster turns on his heel and marches out of the room, not sparing me another word. I sit there for a long minute, trying to breathe before I get up and clean myself off.

I'm too shocked by the abrupt ending to really draw any conclusions, but I do know one thing.

I just had my first sexual encounter.

And it was... Well, it was definitely *something*.

10

KATHERINE

I'm on my own again for the next few days. I don't know where Monster is, and no one communicates with me. The maids glare at me with suspicious eyes every time I see them.

I guess that's my penance for stealing their stuff.

Wandering the halls of the mansion aimlessly, I find myself replaying the events of the other day over and over again. Specifically, I remember the moment when I sat up and looked him in the eye.

I try to understand the mercurial emotions that passed between us just then. Anger and rage. Lust. But there was more than that.

Perhaps there was attraction, coming from me and from him?

I don't understand it and I definitely do not like it. Or him.

But it was there nonetheless.

I consider trying to divorce the idea of him, from the concept of what he's done. Yes, he's a kidnapper, a murderer, a torturer.

But when I picture him in my mind's eye, I think of his smooth muscles and big frame. I think of the way his black button-up shirts are just a little snug, pulling a bit at the chest and on his biceps.

And after his display the other day, I can't help but think of his big... *package*. It was huge, as thick as a soda can and twice as long.

I'd be lying if I said that I hadn't lain in bed, trying to figure out how his penis was supposed to... to *fit* inside any woman's vagina.

It just seems so wrong and impossible that God would create a man so... destructive. Taking away Monster's personality, take away his misdeeds. Just having a penis like that...

Like it was made to ruin whatever poor woman caught Monster's attention.

That seemed really cruel, from the get-go. Like God was laughing at whatever fly was caught in Monster's web.

And since I am currently the fly flitting around the outsides of that web, I have good reason to worry.

I would be also lying if I said that I didn't imagine how he would fit inside my body. Not that I want that, of course. It looks *painful*. But I had that thought all the same.

During the afternoons, I walk in the yard, trailed by Sin and the other guards. I spend my time memorizing the tall stonework fence, staring at every little crack, trying to make myself remember the main defects.

Because I don't intend to be here forever. I'm not sure how long it will take Monster to grow bored with me. Nor am I certain what he will do then. Rape and murder are on the top of the list of things I'm worried about, though.

I am definitely not going to stick around and see if Monster just changes his mind on a whim, though. When the time comes that I need to be ready to flee... assuming that there is even a moment when Sin or the maids aren't looking right at me... I'll be ready to go.

I try talking to Sin, but he just stares off into the distance as if I'm not here. Eventually, I leave Sin and the bodyguards behind in the afternoon heat, in favor of wandering around inside the house.

I've never spent so much time not doing anything. At home, I was always doing laundry or scrubbing floors or cooking something for someone. While I don't miss doing those things much, I am at a loss for what I'm supposed to do.

What do I do? By the end of the third day alone, with no one to speak to, I'm at my wit's end. I invent little games for myself, as a way of staying sane.

I wander through the empty rooms, betting myself whether or not I can find any lost items from the people that used to live here. Because it's obvious enough that a family used to live here.

I can tell by certain details. The small notches carved into a doorframe to chart someone's growth. The scratches on the floor in a large, bright room that I imagine used to be a living room. The light marks in an arc pattern indicate a rocking horse, maybe.

Okay, so I don't know what kind of activity they are proof of, but I like to think that the family that used to live here was healthy and vital. I spend a little time wondering how many children were here, and how old they were.

How did Monster come to own this house? What happened to the family that lived here?

I find a room that used to be a library, with soaring built-in bookshelves and a bricked-over fireplace. The room is down by the locked rooms in what I've come to think of as the east wing. I like the library, for all its empty shelves. All the wood bookshelves are brightly polished and so well-hewn. It feels warm somehow, as if it was once cherished and well-kept by someone.

As I'm exploring the bookshelves, looking for any bit of information to feed my curious mind, I find something.

On the edge of one of the tall bookshelves, tucked off to the side, there is a little lever. I glance around to make sure no one is watching, holding my breath, then I push up on the lever.

I hear gears grinding somewhere behind the bookshelf, and then the frigging wall *moves*. I back up as it opens a few inches, giving a long-suffering sigh.

I think I accidentally opened a secret passage of some kind!

My eyes are wide and my fingers trembling as I pry at the opening. I have to really pull at it to get the bookshelf to move, but soon a dark hallway is partially illuminated by the sunlight in the library.

Unable to resist the lure of something new and different to break up my day, I slip inside. As soon as I'm inside, I immediately sneeze. There's a thick layer of dust on the floor, several inches at least.

Apparently, no one has used this passage for a long, long time.

The passage is probably only three feet wide and perhaps twenty feet long. I creep forward, putting my hands out when it gets too dark to see in front of my face. I stumble over something lying on the floor, maybe a stack of books or magazines.

When I reach the other end of the passage, I find a broad, flat door. There is a smooth wooden handle that I pull down on, which releases a latch on the other side. The gears start grinding, and then suddenly I'm in a room I've never seen before.

The walls are all black, the room itself dimly lit by only a parted curtain. I can tell that it is definitely a bedroom. There is a big bed, draped in black silk and a couple of bedside tables. Other than a door that probably leads to an adjoining bathroom, a sleek black cabinet for clothing storage, and a plain wooden bookshelf that matches the ones I just saw in the library, the room in empty.

Shit! I suddenly put a couple of things together in my head and realize whose bedroom I am probably inside.

Monster's bedroom.

A laugh bubbles to my lips, even as I realize how dangerous being in here is. It strikes me as funny for some reason, finding Monster's place of refuge. There is a joke to be made about how he must not be a vampire after all, but who would I make it to?

The black walls stare back at me, seeming to taunt me. The thought occurs to me that this could be Sin's bedroom or one of the other bodyguards, but...

There is something about this room that just shouts *Monster* to me. I can't resist sneaking forward into the room, running my fingertips over the black silk sheets of his bed.

I leave the whisper of silk behind in favor of Monster's bedside table. I go over to it, biting my lip and crinkling my brow when I see a picture of Monster in the French Quarter. I pick up the picture gently, staring at Monster looking happy, posing with a slim-hipped brunette. I examine the woman clinging to him tightly, realizing with a start that she and I look very much alike, except for our hair.

Mostly just in our faces, and the way we carry ourselves. In an expensive and pricy black lace dress, it's obvious that she's dressed much flashier than me. She wears a pair of sky-high heels and clutches a tiny black purse.

But nothing could disguise the dark circles under her eyes or the hint of whipped dog displayed in her bearing. It makes me wonder who she is, where she's from.

And just what she's doing on the arm of my kidnapper, grinning and posing.

I cautiously put the frame back and slip open the drawer below. There are a few papers at the bottom and a small blue bottle of unlabeled white pills, but nothing that sheds any light on who Monster is.

I close the drawer and look around. The bookshelf calls to me, and I pad over to it. Most of the books have spines in a different alphabet. I squint, recognizing a few letters. I think they're Greek.

That makes sense. Monster's heavy foreign accent, his olive complexion, his black hair... it all squares with the notion that he might be Greek.

There are a few titles that are in English, though... *Atlas Shrugged, The Count of Monte Cristo, A Clockwork Orange, Catcher in The Rye, Heart of Darkness, The Road,* and *The Prince*. I haven't read most of those books, but I sense a pattern emerging. All of those books are about hopelessness or insanity. A lot of death.

I get a chill, just reading the titles. I spot a huge compendium of Shakespeare on Monster's bookshelf, the volume very well-thumbed. That one throws me for a loop.

So, even monsters read Shakespeare? Interesting.

I hear a faint sound from somewhere outside of the bedroom, like a footfall in the long hallway. In an instant, I whisk myself away to the open panel of Monster's bedroom. Careful to close the door very quietly, I sneak down the little hallway in perfect darkness.

Though I want to spend some time exploring the hallway and whatever reading materials might be on the floor there, there's no time. I scurry down the passage and out from behind the bookcase, closing it with a definitive clink.

Somewhere, gears grind again, but I'm not worried about that. I stand stock still and wait, heart racing. Monster storms by the open door, not even glancing my way. He looks more than a little angry, shouting in his native tongue to another man that looks like he could be Monster's clone.

Oh, shit. There are two of them out there in the world? My blood runs cold.

For some reason, the fact that Monster has a brother or a cousin does nothing to humanize him. It just chills me to the bone. The idea that there are more people like *him*.

My breath freezes in my chest. All I can do is flatten myself against the wall and pray that I don't give myself away. As soon as they leave the hallway, I silently creep down out of the library and down the hall, heading for the relative safety of my bedroom.

11

ARSEN

"It doesn't matter!" I hiss at my brother, as we enter my room. "The Carollas may be dead, but their street-level dealers are still clinging to the idea that they will be back someday. And this big deal with the Columbians was supposed to go through today, but now it's fucking ruined because of those fucking bastards."

I rip my black button-up off over my head, seething. I'm frustrated beyond belief, unwilling to even believe that the city of New Orleans would bother to mourn the Carollas. From everything I have heard, they treated everyone around them like shit.

So, why should their dealers feel any loyalty to them? Especially, when I came in after the Carollas disappeared and waved fat stacks of cash around?

Money is all that matters to anyone. The sooner the city of New Orleans learns that lesson, the better. In the meantime, I'm having to take meetings with cartels and watch other mafia bosses start to eye the city I just cleared out.

That city is *mine*. And I'll do whatever I have to do to

make it my bitch, even if that means starving it of dope and fresh girls.

I crack my knuckles, pissed the fuck off. Damen looks at me, his expression bored.

"Are you done with your hissy fit yet?" he asks.

I roll my eyes at him. "This little display of defiance is costing us a million dollars a day. Not just me, *us*. You would do better to care more."

I walk over to the closet, choosing a fresh shirt. Damen says nothing, which is normal. The three of us have long since learned to shut our mouths when someone else is angry. You would be surprised what a man will tell you about himself in a fit of pique.

I turn, suddenly noticing that the picture on my bedside table has been moved. The silver frame catches the sunlight from this direction, where it normally wouldn't. I walk over to my bedside table, fury building in me like a powder keg, ready to go off.

One of the finest arts I've learned over the past decade has been not expecting the fireworks to go off. It is more a matter of choosing when they will go off, and who will witness my explosive font of anger.

I straighten the frame with two fingers. I want to rant and rave maniacally at the maids, punish whichever particular one they point the finger at when I demand to know who cleaned my room. But I won't do that.

No, not when I have another victim so close at hand. One that is small and blonde and just waiting breathlessly for my punishments to begin.

Fiore, my little flower. She haunts me, disturbs my sleep. Or perhaps that is Anna's domain; it is hard to tell them apart, hard to distinguish what I might project onto Fiore and what is really just her personality.

I look at Damen, knowing that he wouldn't approve of how I came to acquire Fiore. Not that he has a conscience. He just wouldn't like that I had to pull so many strings to get Fiore. He wouldn't approve of how public I made my quest to get her, how I laid bare my desire to possess her.

"You should go. I have things to do," I say, leaving it at that.

His brow hunches as he stares at me for a few seconds. "What are you up to?"

I wave my hand dismissively. "Lots of things. Don't worry, I can keep myself occupied. I'll let you know what I decide I'm going to do about the Columbian deal."

He gives a small shake of his head, then turns and marches out of my room. I turn toward the doorway, pressing a small button on the wall there. A few seconds later, a tinny voice answers.

"Yes, Senior Aetós?" a woman asks.

I press the button again. "Make sure that my brother makes it out of the house. And I'm going to be busy upstairs. I'm not to be disturbed. Make sure there is no one lurking on the floor."

I release the button. I hear the answering, "Yes, Senior Aetós." I'm not listening to that, though.

No, instead my mind has wandered to Fiore. I'm wondering what she's doing right now, and whether or not she's ready for the agony the I'm about to visit on her.

I dig into the bottom of my closet, rooting around through various boxes of props, until I find a riding crop. I test it against my hand, bending it a little, smiling faintly when the crop bounces back.

Then I pause, dragging the whole box out of the closet. I stand over the box, contemplating. I have whips and harnesses, dildos, and different kinds of gags. I sort through the harnesses, choosing the one made to fit over the hips. Then I grab the magic wand vibrator that can be fitted to the wearer's crotch, grinning to myself.

She has no idea of what I'm capable of, nor does she know what her own body will do when I force her to endure the vibrator, again and again.

I stride out of my room, down the hall toward Fiore's quarters. The way my black boots sound as they echo on the dark wood floors is exciting, their sound hard and merciless; almost everything is exciting to me just now, though.

I haven't seen her in a few days, but I've definitely thought about her. I thought of how small she is; how blonde and petite. I could easily strangle her with my bare hands, any time I want to.

She has to deal with knowing that I could, any time I'm in the room with her.

I thought about how amazing she looked just before I came all over her chest. About how that tiny hint of distaste took over her features for the most fleeting moment.

And most importantly, I fantasized about how it was time to start defiling her. Find out what her desires are. Corrupt those tender feelings, make her lust after the only kind of affection she'll ever get from me.

I'm so far gone into blackness, utterly ruined by a lifetime of violence, fear, and filth. When presented with this innocent, sweet princess I'll do to her the only thing I know how.

I'll shred her innocence, ruin it. Ruin her, forever.

Just like I did with Anna, though I didn't know that I was doing it at the time. At least with Anna, it was more than evident that she longed for death. I saw the track marks on her arms, saw in her eyes that she had a death wish.

Not so with Fiore, or at least not yet. But she will dance

with death. She will know his name and beckon to him like a lover. And then, when she finally begs me for the final release, I'll kill her. Turn my protective embrace into a slow strangulation.

Yes. It's fucked up, but that's the thought that makes my cock hard.

I reach her doorway and find her on her bed, watching me with glittering blue eyes. She expected me to come looking for her, somehow. That fact is satisfying to me, although it will be better when she waits with a smile.

Right now, her expression is one of dread. I see her gaze shift to the items in my hands. Her eyebrow lifts delicately as she tries to figure out what I have in store for her.

I stride over to her, looming over her small frame. I can see from her eyes that she wants to run, but she doesn't. She knows better than that by now.

She straightens her spine as well as she can, her expression pinched. Little does she know; her expression is filling my chest with renewed vigor. I lean over, dropping the magic wand and harness on the bed before her.

"Have you missed me, my Fiore?" I ask, my voice a low rumble. I put a hand on her shoulder, trying not to grin when she flinches. She's so small and delicate, her skin as white as porcelain against my darker hand. I caress her shoulder, dropping my touch down to her breast.

"No," she says. "I haven't missed you at all."

I cover her breast with my hand, shaping the handful of flesh. She takes a trembling breath, dropping my gaze. I pinch her nipple through the cloth of her dress, tweaking it until she cries out.

"I think it's time that I taught you to be civil," I murmur. "This time, when I leave you for a few days, you'll have something to remember me by."

Planting one of my hands on her warm thighs, I pull her down to the end of the bed, to make her easier to reach. Taking my time, I run my hands up her thighs and shape her hips. An audible gasp leaves her lips when I rip open her dress, rending the garment from her collarbone right down past her thighs.

Her features all seem to freeze as I explore her naked body with my fingertips, caressing her breasts. As I make my way down her body, over her taut belly, she clenches her thighs closed. One corner of my mouth lifts.

If she thinks that clenching will stop me from getting what I want, she has another think coming. Her eyes widen when I reach for the harness that I brought.

"What is that for?" she asks, fear blossoming to life in her eyes.

"Nothing sinister," I say casually. "But if you don't let me put it on you, there will be a severe punishment."

She swallows and lies still for me as I slide the harness up her legs and fasten it around her hips and thighs. Picking up the magic wand vibrator, I point it at her.

"Have you used one of these on yourself before?" I ask, my tone almost gentle.

A confused look crosses Fiore's features. "Used it for what?"

I almost groan with excitement, because it seems she hasn't ever even seen one. Flipping the ON button at the base, I let it purr on the lowest setting. Her eyes get even wider when I touch her inner thigh with the wand, pressing it against her flash hard enough to make a white mark.

"I... I really don't know what all this is for," she says, squirming a little.

"This?" I ask, spreading her legs. She gasps at the invasion of me opening her legs. The vibrator in my hand travels to the nest of curls, teasing her skin everywhere but on her pussy. "This is so that when I'm gone, you think about me. There will be a little ache between your legs that won't go away anytime soon. I want you to long for someone to touch that pretty little pussy of yours. I want you to picture my face, picture my hands, or my cock, giving you what you need."

She attempts to close her legs again, so I bring my hand up to her neck, giving it a gentle squeeze. It feels as though my hand was meant to fit there, nestled against the fine lines of her delicate neck. That feeling of being made to fit makes me hard, makes me grind my cock against her hip.

"Don't resist me," I warn her, an undercurrent of violence in my words. I squeeze her neck for emphasis. "Just let this happen. It will go much more smoothly for you if you are a good girl."

She looks fucking scared, which only makes me harder. Releasing her neck, I slowly push her knees up, which gives me a clear view of her sweet little pussy. Using two fingers to spread her pussy lips wide, I bring the wand down to kiss her clit.

The first touch of the wand makes her try to curl inward, like a clam closing its shell. She makes an almost inaudible gasp.

"Don't," I warn her, reaching over to weigh one of her breasts in my palm. Tweaking her nipple a little, I'm rewarded with her opening to me once more. The vibrator hums in my hand, the sound steady as I start working it in tight little circles.

I push my cock against the back of her thigh, the fabric between me and her starting to irritate me. When I step back, and the vibrator leaves her clit, she makes an odd sound. Not quite a moan, but something close to a whimper.

"Are you starting to like what I'm doing to you, Fiore?" I ask, using the harness to hold the vibrator in place against her flesh.

She bites her lip, resisting whatever emotion she doesn't want to show. She closes her eyes for a moment, but she can't hide the blush that has started on her cheeks or the way her chest rises and falls a little faster.

This time when I step away, the vibrator continues its work without me. Unzipping my pants, I get my cock out, fisting it. It's hard and long; covered in veins. Eyeing Fiore, I slap her on the ass with my free hand.

She lets her eyes flutter open. Her expression upon seeing me standing over her with my hand on my hard cock... if I could write poems about it, I would. She's surprised and yet, aroused. I can tell from one look at her.

I reach out and press the vibrator into her clit a little harder, stroking my cock with my free hand. To see her like this, tied up and vulnerable... especially, after the last few days of hellish business I've been conducting in New Orleans...

I'm more than a little excited to see my girl, all primed and ready for me. She looks so hot like that, all trussed and prepared to receive whatever I've got to give her. Basically, I can finish anywhere I want, I just have to decide where that is.

Getting onto the bed, I flip her over so that she's on her elbows and knees, ass up in the air. I can't see her face this way, but I can hear the breathy sounds she's making. Looking at her like this, her perfect ass so exposed, her pussy tormented by the vibrator...

I let a groan loose as I stroke my cock and think about how much I want her pussy touching my cock, milking me. Or her mouth, her pink lips sucking at my cock until it's dry.

She trembles before me, right on the verge of orgasm. I get closer to her, the tip of my dick prodding her ass. She moans as her whole body clenches.

"You're going to come, aren't you?" I mutter to her, hammering my fist on my cock. "You are a very, very bad girl. God, you're going to make me come too."

She stills for a second as if she has a choice. Then she starts to call out. "Oh... oh... oh god... oh..."

As quick as that, I lose control of myself, gushing my seed all over her ass. I thrust against her ass a few times, making sure every drop is wrung from my cock.

Immediately disgusted with myself and my poor self-control, I straighten myself up and clamber off the bed. I tuck my cock back into my pants, admiring the traces of cum I left on her ass. If it were possible to tattoo that on her ass permanently, I would.

I flick the button of the magic wand off, then turn and leave. She can figure out what to do with the wand and the harness. I have more important things that I should be doing.

12

ARSEN

There is something bothering me, a niggling sensation in the back of my mind that just won't go away. I know it has to do with Fiore. It must.

If I'm honest with myself, which I normally am, I spend entirely too much time and energy focused on her when I'm here. It's kind of sickening, how much easier it is to obsess over her budding sexuality than it is to worry about whatever problems I have back in New Orleans.

There is a whole empire waiting for me there, with all the challenges and stress of any growing republic. Here, though?

Here, there is only *her*. It's much simpler to wonder if I can make her actually enjoy the blend of pleasure mixed with pain that I savor. Or maybe, being as inexperienced as she seems to be, she will just assume that everything I do is normal. That what I like is normal.

Shit, maybe I can permanently hardwire her to need pain in order to come. That would give me the ultimate rush, knowing that I had done something so everlasting. I could create the perfect little sex toy, ready for and excited to be dominated by me.

Now that is an interesting thought.

It's not as if she ever really goes away, either. I've got her trapped here indefinitely, just waiting on me. Even now, I feel her presence in the hallway across from my bedroom. As I stand there, unlocking the door to my personal office, I know without a doubt that I have an audience.

"Fiore!" I call, twisting the doorknob. "I know you're there. You might as well come out."

Her blonde head peeks out from the shining blue-papered wall, where the hallway turns. I see her curious blue eyes, see the swirl of emotions set there.

Cautious, guarded, nosy. Starved for input from the outside world.

Opening the door with a sweeping gesture, I invite her to see what she so clearly wants to see. My office, where I conduct most of my business when I'm here.

A huge cedar desk in front of a huge wall of books. A pair of plain, straight-backed chairs faces the desk. In the corner, a comfortable leather chair looks out over the mansion's courtyard.

I glance at Fiore, who is slowly making her way down the corridor. I've taken away her shoes and her choice of clothes. I've had her hair dyed to remove the flashy bright blonde. I've done dirty things to her, marked her with lashes of my cum.

And yet, she seems above it. Her posture is still frail and nervous like she's expecting a violent outburst at any moment.

But there is something in the way that she conducts herself. An elegance to the way she carries her head so high. Something I didn't see clearly before.

"Come on, then," I say, jerking my head toward the open door. "You know you want to look."

Heading into my office, I make my way around to my desk, sitting in my comfortable black rolling chair. Fiore appears in the doorway, hesitating. I can feel her eyes on my book collection on the wall behind me.

Opening my laptop on my desk, I sift through a handful of emails while she decides if she's going to enter the room or not. When she does, tiptoeing inside and pausing by one of the stiff-backed wooden chairs, she looks like a deer ready to take flight.

I favor her with a glance. "What is it that you want, Fiore?"

She blushes, tucking a strand of hair behind her ear. Her eyes are glued to the books behind my head. I have to try not to take it personally that she doesn't actually want to be in the room with me. It's the books that she lusts after.

She doesn't say anything, just stares at them, chewing on her lips nervously.

"Sit down," I say, pointing to the chair.

She looks at me, her blue eyes locking on my face, and I can almost hear her pulse pick up. She slides her body around to the front of the chair, almost seeming unwilling to take the risk of sitting here with me.

It's sort of satisfying to know that the system I've been training her with — the stripping away of her identity, then rebranding her by alternately tormenting her and playing nice — is working.

She swallows, and her eyes are drawn back to the books again. Rocking back in my chair, I contemplate her. It would be nothing for me to give her a book... but I want something in return.

What should I demand, though?

The fact that I haven't yet ground her old life out of her mind weighs on me. As long as she still thinks that there is a chance that someone might save her, life won't be completely restful for me. Better that she gives up on it entirely.

"You want a book to read?" I say, gesturing behind me.

Her eyes widen for a second, then she swallows again and nods. "Yes."

I cock my head, considering her. "You weren't randomly chosen to be my toy. There is a reason, which has everything to do with the men who were part of your family. You know that, right?"

A puzzled look appears on her face, her brow puckering just a tiny bit. "I know that... I mean I *assume* that you are a rival of my father's."

That is more right than she knows. I don't think that she knows that her father is dead, though. It takes me a few seconds to make sure that my next words are well-considered.

"Correct. What I don't think you understand is how vile and corrupt your family was. I think they sheltered you from a lot." I stop, a thought occurring to me. "Obviously, not too much though, since they fucking sold you."

She blanches and reels like she's been hit, biting her lip. She doesn't say anything, but her expression grows more intense.

"I just want to make sure that you fully understand something, Fiore. I want you to realize that you're dead to them. They are not coming to save you. And you shouldn't want them to, honestly. For all my flaws, I think I have saved you from them."

A scowl immediately overtakes her face. When she

speaks, her tone is terse, as if she's spitting. "You're no savior."

My brows rise. "No? You think not?"

"I know better," she says, her jaw jutting out stubbornly.

"I think you're wrong. Not only that, but I have a video that you should see. It's time that the blinders come off. It's time to see your family for who they really are."

A perplexed look crosses her face. "You have a video of them?"

"I do. And I'll show it to you."

She looks suspicious. "What if I don't want to see it?"

I roll backward, glancing at the wall of books. "I'll trade you. One book for one minute of viewing. That's more than fair, I think."

Her lip curls a bit in defiance. "Like you would know what is and is not *fair*."

"Do you not want the book, then?" I say, pretending to rise from my chair.

"I didn't say that," she says quickly.

"Because it's a good deal."

She presses her lips together, repressing whatever she wants to say. A soft smile plays on my lips. She's learning.

"It's a generous offer. Go ahead and pick any book you like." I gesture to the wall behind me. "Or you can go back to memorizing the ceiling tiles or whatever it is that you do when I'm not here."

That earns me a glare, but she doesn't argue. She just stands up, watching me carefully, and comes around to my side of the desk. I spend the next couple of minutes looking at her body. Her long legs, her firm breasts, that fucking ass...

Her ass is amazing. Flawless. Without reproach. As she

creeps by my chair, trying to pick the best book possible, I casually reach out and grab a handful of her sweet ass.

"Hey!" she squeaks, slapping at my hand.

"It's mine. I'll touch it if I want to," I shrug, moving my hand back.

She darts away, evading my touch. "How about *The Count of Monte Cristo*?"

Wheeling toward my bookshelf, I see a copy of the novel there. "If that is your choice, then certainly."

Fiore makes strong eye contact with me, like that will stop me from groping her while she reaches for the book.

"Uh-uh," I tell her, reaching out and grabbing her by the hips. She writhes away from my touch, a protest already on her lips. "We agreed. You have to watch it first."

Giving me the evil eye, she scurries around the desk, hovering on the other side. "Fine."

I smirk at her. She thinks that she is playing a game, but I'm the king. I make the rules. I could have her every day and every night if I wanted to take her by force. Bent over this damn desk, if that was what made me hard.

Turning to my laptop, I click a few buttons. A black video viewing screen pops up, and I turn the whole computer away from me. I've already seen this video of Sal Carolla and his sons raping and killing Anna enough times.

The hour has come for Fiore to understand just how deviant and perverted her own family was. Then, when I've let that sink in for a while, I'll let her know that I killed those fuckers before I ever even bought her.

It's a slow game that I'm playing, but ever so worthwhile.

I mute the volume and press play, watching Fiore's face. The video cuts right to Sal balls deep inside Anna, with Anna screaming and pleading for mercy. Fiore's eyes widen, and she glances up at me. Perhaps waiting for confirmation that this is all a joke.

But it isn't a joke. This video was dropped off at my New Orleans residence after Anna's head, to rub salt in my wounds. Actually, you could say that this video was what made me decide to kill them all.

All but my Fiore. Her, I kept alive, just waiting for moments like this.

Moments where I swear, I can see her heart actually shredding into a million pieces. Her complexion takes on a faintly green cast, and she staggers away from the computer.

She looks at me, her blue eyes filled with horror and disgust. She gasps out a single word. "Why?"

But before I can respond, she races out of the room, trying to get as far away as possible from what she's just seen. The images are inside her mind now, though. Just like they're in my head.

Burned permanently.

I sit back, putting my hands behind my head and looking out the window.

Now she knows, at least.

I'm not the only man in her life that is capable of evil.

13

KATHERINE

There's a series of broad clay steps that lead from the backyard to the front. Tucked away on the side of the mansion, winding gently around the kitchen and laundry, no one goes over there. It's a little scenic, with trees clustered overhead. I can even make out the nearby mountains from this spot, so it's a perfect place to reflect.

Today, even Sin and the other bodyguards are missing in action, so it's just me alone on the steps. My arms are wrapped around my knees as I stare out into the misty tree line, lost in my own thoughts.

Mainly, I'm homesick today. I know that all the shit has been going on here recently, and I have plenty of things to be concerned about. Not the least of which is Monster himself. He seems unhinged lately.

That doesn't spell anything good for me, I'm afraid. But beyond Monster's moods, beyond being kidnapped and brought here against my will, there's more. There is a sadness that has seeped deep down in my bones. New Orleans calling out to my very blood itself.

I think of my brothers when they were young and still

sweet. When I was a little girl, I was homeschooled; told that it was for my protection. So, I would wait by the door for when my brothers would get home, anxiously waiting for some news from the outside world.

My brothers would pile in the door wearing their red and grey prep school uniforms, and each of them would touch my head.

"Hey, Kat," each of them would say.

Usually, if I was good, Tony would even bring me a piece of Roman taffy and a story about his day. That's how I grew up, through Tony's candy and stories. When Mom died, Tony got me a bunch of that Roman taffy and a box full of books.

Shakespeare, Harper Lee, F. Scott Fitzgerald, Ray Bradbury... all were jammed inside that box. Tony didn't know it, but that box of books started my love affair with the written word. It's how I got out of my home and explored the deepest jungles and rode jagged ice floes.

Thinking about that right now, about the books and my once-beloved Tony, my eyes fill with tears. I lay my head down on my knees and close my eyes.

The need to sob is strangely absent. Maybe it's the fact that the last time I saw Tony, he was literally handing me over to kidnappers.

And then there's my father. The man I was supposed to love for my whole life. The man who was supposed to protect me, no matter what. He betrayed me, sold me, stuck me *here*.

And let's not forget that I saw that video of him... *hurting* that girl. How can I be expected to forget or forgive something like that?

I can't. I won't. All I can do is harden myself against the facts now.

Maybe it's how far away New Orleans seems, full of problems that are impossibly small compared with what I have to deal with now.

Either way, I just sit there for a long time. I let my tears flow unchecked for the time being, not know or caring whether they were for my family or for me. The breeze blows gently, stirring my hair.

The wind shifts. I get a sense that I should open my eyes. When I do, I'm startled to find someone sitting not two feet away. How did he get there so quickly and quietly?

And he's not just anyone, either. There can be no doubt that it's Monster's brother, staring at me intently with those eerie grey eyes. Like Monster, he's well over six feet tall, and made of pure muscle. My gaze is drawn to his hands, powerful and deft.

He flexes them unconsciously, and I start to wonder how many women just like me he has hurt with his hands alone. Those hands are a kind of beautiful danger. That much I'm sure of.

There is something about him though... something in his eyes, like a predator scenting his prey perhaps. It sets me on edge right away. I look back at him, and my breathing grows uneven.

He smiles playfully, which gives me chills all over my body. "You are prettier than I thought you would be, Katherine. My brother doesn't appreciate that about you."

I want to ask why he would use my real name when I've heard nothing but *Fiore* from Monster these past two weeks. I want to tell him to take his compliments and shove them somewhere unpleasant.

But I don't. Instead, I just suspiciously blurt out the first thing that comes to mind.

"Who are you? Are you... *his* brother?"

He nods slowly. "Yes. I'm Damen. I'm just here while my brother transacts some business. I thought I would check on his investment, see how you're faring under my brother's tutelage."

Why does every word he speaks fill me with a sense of dread?

"What do you want?" I demand to know.

His expression turns patient. He looks at me like a cat looks at a mouse like he's bored but he might as well practice chasing me.

"I want many things," he says, reaching out to trail his fingertips along the flesh above my knee. I recoil, pushing myself away from him.

"Don't touch me," I warn. "I will scream for the guards."

He laughs. "I like that you believe there are guards here for your protection. You realize that those men are here to keep you from escaping, right?"

I lift my chin. "I don't think they will like *you* touching me."

He cocks a brow, infuriatingly smug.

"That doesn't really matter, because I sent them on an errand outside of the compound. See, I think that you and I should spend some time getting to know each other." He leans toward me, gripping my knee so hard that it's painful. "You've shown my brother a good time. Now it's my turn."

"Stop," I warn him, backing away. "I haven't shown anybody anything, and I don't want you to touch me."

He climbs to his feet, dusting himself off. "Do you think that matters to me? It only makes me want to make it fucking hurt, you stupid little slut."

My heart begins to hammer incredibly fast. I need to *run*.

There is a second where I try to measure the distance

down the stairs, try to figure out how I can play the angles to my advantage. I take a second too long to decide to run down the stairs, and he's already moving toward me as I start to turn.

I only make it a few steps when he catches the back of my dress, ripping the fabric a little. I scream as he grabs me by the arm, spinning me around. I lose my balance and fall backward. He doesn't stop me but instead, surges forward so that we both land in the hard-packed dirt that lines the steps.

I hit the ground with a smack, and he lands on top of me. My legs part, cushioning him, cradling his big body. For a second, I'm paralyzed by the fact that I hit my head on the ground. I blink up at Damen, my mouth opens a little, dazed.

His weight on my body is undeniable, but it's so surreal to me that I'm lying here on the ground, beneath a strange man.

Damen doesn't pull any punches. While I'm frozen, he's already shoving my shift up my legs and unzipping his pants. I catch a glimpse of his penis -- long, thick, and veiny.

It's only then that reality is kick-started for me once more, and I start to scream and struggle.

"No! No, don't touch me!" I yell, my hands scratching at his face.

He laughs, very low and sinister, and grabs me by the hair. "You talk too damn much."

"No!" I scream again, but it is muffled by his mouth on mine, his tongue invading my mouth.

I can feel his hard penis pressed against my thigh, oozing some sort sticky fluid. He thrusts violently against my thighs and sticks his tongue down my throat. I choke and gasp for breath as I keep fighting against him. Even though the voice in the back of my head is saying that it's no use, that anyone as big as he is will win every time, I still struggle.

"No!" I cry as he tries to get my thighs open. He wrestles with me, yanking my hair. I scream at the pain of it.

"You think you're too good for my cock, huh? We'll see who wins," he grunts. "You'll take everything I have to give you, and you'll thank me for it. That's what good girls do."

He shoves his free hand down between my legs and puts three of his cool fingers into my vagina, which makes me cry out again. At the blunt brutality of it, at the suddenness and shock, I feel. He scissors his fingers into my most sensitive flesh, making me worried that he will somehow tear me apart.

A strangled sound of shock comes from my throat as he leans forward and shoves his tongue down my throat again. I bite down on his tongue as hard as I can, which seems to surprise him. He reels back and then punches me in the side of the head. Everything goes blurry. I feel a white wave of pulsing agony spread out from the middle of my head, covering my skull and even my shoulders.

I hear a voice in the distance, calling out. A male...

No, not just any voice.

Monster's voice.

He is screaming at Damen in their mother tongue, ripping Damen away from me. Damen responds, angry. Monster pushes Damen and gets in his face, but I don't care for their argument. My mind is too busy spinning its wheels, trying to piece together what has just happened to me.

I curl up in a ball, pulling the tattered pieces of my dress back together. A broken sob escapes me as I try to protect my head and my violated body the best I can.

"Fucking cunt," Damen screams, spitting in my direction. "I hope that you need my help soon, brother. I can't wait to deny you as you have denied me."

"I brought her. I get to claim her first," Monster says, infuriated.

My blood runs cold at the idea that Monster is only saving me so that he can do the exact same thing to me.

Damen sneers, spits at me, and then storms off. Monster looks over at me on the ground, his chest heaving. I shiver and close my arms around my legs, squeezing my eyes closed.

I expect Monster to just leave me here, to storm off angrily. But he doesn't. Instead, he picks me up as carefully as if I am made of glass, cradling me in his arms.

He doesn't say a word. He just heads inside the mansion, his expression set in a determined grimace. I let myself lean into him a little, let myself cry against his starched button up shirt.

He carries me up the stairs like it's no big deal. Like I weigh nothing at all. He puts me on my bed, gracefully pulling the tatters of my dress off. I don't resist. I don't do anything except to sit here, feeling an ocean of numbness rising and churning within me.

Monster disappears into my bathroom for a second, returning with a damp washcloth. As he runs it over my legs and my belly, I close my eyes. Right now, it's the closest thing I'm going to get to a caress.

Even though it's Monster, I will take whatever small crumbs he's willing to offer. Just now, just at this moment. I lean into his touch, tears tracking slowly down my face.

When he's satisfied that I am clean, he puts me in a clean dress, wriggling the thing down over my head. I lie down with a sigh, wiping away tears.

"That won't ever happen again," he says quietly, looking away. He's still angry, but I don't think it's me he has a quarrel with. Then he pins me with his gaze, his grey eyes searching my face. "You're for me, you understand? My property. Nobody is fucking stupid enough to harm something that belongs to me."

I just lie there, desensitized to everything.

What does it even matter?

What does any of it matter?

Closing my eyes, I shut out the rest of the world.

He keeps talking to me, but I just squeeze my eyes and wish harder.

Go away.

Go the hell away!

Eventually, he does. I fall asleep finally, and when I wake up, there is a comforter at the end of my bed. I kick it away, not in the mood for any kind of apology, no matter who it's from.

14

KATHERINE

Monster is gone for a week or more this time. I can't say that I miss him. I'm still reeling over the video he forced me to watch.

A blindfolded and gagged girl, being brutally raped by my own father. What's more, I recognized the girl. It was the girl from the picture beside Monster's bed.

Several pieces clicked into place for me in that moment, but it mostly highlighted what I still did not know.

Who was the girl?

How was she connected to Monster?

And mostly, how could anyone do what my father did to that girl? It was the most foul treatment of another human being that I could think of.

I never wanted to know any of that. So, I'm furious at my whole family for being the scum of the earth, yes. But I'm also pissed off at Monster for making me aware of the whole thing.

In this one instance, I think I would have preferred not to know. Now even if I had dreamed of being rescued by my family in some sort of dream scenario, I don't know if I would go with them. Or rather, I'd let them take me out of here, and then I would promptly flee their custody.

And the book that I traded my lack of knowledge for? It's lying right beside me in my bed. I spent about three hours trying not to read it. Then I gave in...

And I'm kind of glad that I did.

Whatever else is going on, there is nothing like the classic escapism that comes from reading a good book. It's been many years since I read *The Count of Monte Cristo*, but I'm sucked in immediately. It's hard not to read it all in one sitting, but I force myself to read slowly. I consider the words on each page for a nice long time before I turn to the next.

When Monster finally returns though, I know it. Everyone in the whole house knows it. He announces his presence by snapping demands at the maids and screaming instructions at one of the bodyguards.

I float around the edges of his frenzied activity, watching a maid scurry from his private office, tears in her eyes. He bellows commands in a different language and expects the house staff to jump to his commands.

It's not particularly pretty, but it is sort of fun to watch. Even Sin gets yelled at, berated for some minor thing. My lips curve up as I watch Sin leave Monster's office with a deadly look on his face.

Though I don't want the attention, I know that it's only a matter of time before Monster remembers that I'm here. Most of his day is spent angrily arguing with people on the phone, but I don't expect it to last.

Returning to my room, I keep my head down and don't make waves. Maybe I'll just weather this storm with no problems if I'm quiet enough.

When has my life ever gone so well, though?

It's late by the time that Monster appears in my doorway, rolling up his sleeves. His expression is nothing short of forbidding, signaling a rocky road ahead for me. I sit up, swallowing against the lump that forms in my throat and hug my bare knees.

When my eyes make contact with his, I feel a direct current running between us. He's a live wire, stripped of any sort of protection. Monster looks at me dispassionately as he strolls into my room.

"Get undressed," he orders, his voice throaty.

Causing tension when I already know Monster's in a bad mood isn't high on my list priorities, but what am I supposed to do? I greet him anxiously, putting my legs down on the floor, with a quivering hand in the air.

"Monster, I know that you're upset--" I start, but he cuts me off.

His expression hardens. "Shut up. I'm not interested in what you have to say. I'm interested in your body, and how you're going to use it to get me off."

He unbuckles his belt, which makes my eyes go wide. Surely, he won't whip me with his belt. I didn't even do anything wrong!

Unless he found out about the secret passage, that is.

A shiver wracks my whole body.

He doesn't seem concerned though. He tosses his belt to the floor and begins unbuttoning his shirt. I feel the electric contact of his eyes, piercing me and stabbing me. He growls at the fact that I seem frozen, gawking at him.

"You have until I get this shirt off to get naked. Don't make me tell you again."

This is it. This is the moment that I've been dreading when he finally decides that he's tired of playing around.

He's going to have sex with me, to put his giant dick inside my small body, and he's not even going to warm me up first.

A cold sweat breaks out over my body as I lift my dress up over my head with shaking hands. He looks at me, his grey eyes calculating as he steps up to the bed. Flushing all the way to my roots, I try to cover myself with my hands.

I feel more naked standing here now than I've ever felt.

Am I tall enough?

Am I too scrawny to turn anyone on?

Are my breasts big enough?

Is my ass too big?

While I'm doubting myself, he's taking off his shirt, leaving him stripped bare to the waist. He's in amazing physical shape, his pecs muscular and flat while his biceps are impressively large and veiny. His abs are hard, and he even has that vee of muscle that narrows to his hips.

Everything else about him aside, Monster is friggin ripped. He's hot, and there is no denying it. He may very well live up to his moniker, but damn if I don't look at him and swoon, just for the barest second.

It's biology. I can't be blamed for that, can I?

Monster looks at me for a second, his eyes narrowing. He reaches out, knocking my hands away, leaving me bare before him. I feel the weight of his gaze as he considers my breasts, my... my *pussy*, and my face, too.

He brushes my hair back behind my ear with the lightest touch. I become aware of my hammering heart only when his fingertips make contact with the shell of my ear, oh so briefly.

Where before he was in a hurry, now he moves languidly, caressing my collarbone in the still-sensitive spot that his knife carved my flesh. Sucking in a breath, I close my eyes against the moment of... not pain, exactly. But not pleasure, either.

What is the word for that?

Excitement? Anticipation?

As I think the words, I judge myself for feeling them. He hurts me. He kidnapped me. He makes me feel unimportant and worthless.

He treats me as if I am a slave.

So why does my heart do a little kick when he touches me? He catches the tip of my breast in his fingertips, massaging it lightly. I squirm a little at the strange sensation he creates and open my eyes.

He moves close enough that we're only a heartbeat away from touching. So that I can feel the heat of his skin. My lips can feel the brush of his warm breath; they part in anticipation, even though I know that it is so very wrong.

Then a throat is cleared. Monster and I both start, turning to look at the doorway. My heart freezes in my chest.

Sin is there, his expression apologetic, filling up the space with his big body. I feel immediate shame that any other person should see me naked. Actually, that anyone should see me so... intrigued by Monster.

"The whole fucking world had better be ending," Monster barks at Sin, looking like he's about to murder him. I consider Sin to be a tough guy, but even he blanches at Monster's words.

He bows his head. "Dryas is here, sir. He has some news about the Sierra Cartel. It's worth interrupting you, sir."

Monster squints at Sin for a moment, then shakes his head. He turns to me.

"Don't think that this is over," he rasps, his expression steely. "It's not even begun."

He turns and marches out of the room, following Sin. And I'm just left, trembling, trying to figure out what the hell just happened.

15

KATHERINE

I'm awakened in the middle of the night by Sin shaking me awake.

"Get up," he says, his expression intense. He releases me, standing back. "The master wants you."

Dazed, I sit up. "What? He wants me *now*?"

His expression turns caustic. "No, I'm just talking to you in the middle the night for fun. This is all a game to me."

Scrunching up my face, I push my wild hair back. "Alright, alright."

I push myself off the bed, moving slowly.

"Come on," Sin says, grabbing me roughly by the arm. He hauls me off the bed and drags me out of my room. "Stop screwing around."

Sin's legs are so much longer than mine, that it's mostly him towing me down the hallway. He heads downstairs and into Monster's private office, where Monster is waiting. The evening air is cool enough for me to feel goosebumps break out all over my body.

I stare at Monster, who is pacing at one end of the office.

I look at the room between us, at the straight-backed chairs and the big oak desk. And then I see Monster's expression, the lazy humor he displays while he waits...

Now I'm *really* worried.

Sin deposits me on the cool wooden floor, vanishing from sight. Monster pins me with his gaze, coming closer.

"I told you we weren't through," he says as if the conversation from two days before was still ongoing. "I warned you, didn't I?"

I open my mouth to respond, but he cuts me off.

"No. I don't need any input from you. What I need is for you to realize your place," he says, seeming almost thoughtful. "I think I've been gone so much recently, that you've been flouncing around here, acting like a spoiled princess. That ends today."

I start to retort. "I didn't do anything."

Monster ignores me, walking over to his desk. He pulls out an elegant black box, the size of his forearm, and sets it on the desk. With a glance up at me, he flips the lid open with one finger.

Inside, there are two gold... *devices*. They are nestled down in black velvet, gleaming in the lamplight, reflecting and refracting the light as I edge closer. One of them straight up looks like a small... *vibrator*. The other one is shaped like an egg, and it appears to have some filmy black material underneath.

Looking up in puzzlement, I cock my head. "I'm sorry, what is going on here exactly?"

He smiles, showing his perfectly white teeth. Picking up the egg with one hand and a small remote with the other, he presses a button. The egg comes to life, vibrating in his open palm. My eyes widen a little as I look up at him.

"You're going to wear this," he explains, brandishing the

vibrator. "I don't believe in taking what isn't mine. That includes your virginity. But I'm still very much a man. And until I can have your virginity, I'm going to seek other pleasures with you. You're going to sit on my lap, and wear this vibrator, and read to me."

"What? No," I scowl. My hands grip my dress, anxiously creating two damp wrinkles in the fabric.

"It's between this and the box beneath your bed." He cocks his head at me. "I could honestly go either way."

My heart starts to race. I quail at the very mention of The Box. "Please! No, not that."

"So, it's the vibrator, then?" He holds up the gold egg so that it gleams in the lamplight.

"I—" I start, then swallow hard. Eyeing the egg, I feel... *dirty*, just looking at it. "I don't know."

He drops the egg back into the box. "It sounds like you want the box."

Claustrophobia threatens to take me over, just thinking about going into The Box by choice. "No! No. I... I'll do whatever it takes to avoid that."

Monster sits down in his office chair, patting his thigh. "Come over here then. Show me you can be a good girl for once."

Biting my lip, I hesitate. If I go to him, if I choose the vibrator over The Box, it's still *my* choice. I would be consenting to it, at least somewhat.

Then again, I didn't choose to be trapped here or to be with Monster.

He lowers his brows. "This is the last time I want to tell you to come over here, Fiore. I can promise you won't like what happens when I stop being nice."

Shaking, I make my way over to Monster on legs that feel like they're made of jelly. He watches me as I slowly make my way over to him, a smile flitting across his features. I stand only inches away from him, looking down at his lap, dreading the contact with him.

"Good girl," he says, reaching out and grabbing my hip. He squeezes it, biting his lip. "You know, if you would just relax, this will be very good for you too."

My only response is a shudder. He grasps my hips, surprising me by twisting me as deftly as a salsa dancer. He turns me around so that I'm bent over his desk, pressed against the solid wood. As I make a noise of protest, he forces my thighs apart with his knee.

"What are you—" I complain until he hikes my dress up to my waist. I'm left perfectly naked, available for his inspection. "Monster!"

I can feel my face burning hot and red. It's so embarrassing, I don't even know what to do with myself.

"Shhhh," he orders, his hands caressing my ass, framing it. "Just be still."

He kneads my ass, running a knuckle down the seam of my body, over my pussy. I squirm as his finger passes over my clit.

It's not that I want him to touch me again, really, it's not.

It's just... my clit *aches*.

What am I supposed to do with that?

A tremor starts deep within my body, and before I know it I'm shaking everywhere. I look back at him over my shoulder, panicking. He seems not to notice, too entranced by his hands on my body.

"Monster—" I try again.

He stops me with a slap on the ass. "That's enough of you. I'll tell you when you can speak again."

Blushing furiously, angry at how he's violating me, I put

my head down on the desk. The sooner I get this over, the better.

"I like when you submit like that," he says. "You know what I like even better?"

I can't speak through the knot in my throat, so I just shake my head. The next second, I'm shocked again when I feel his fingers tease the seam of my pussy.

It's not dry. Actually, more than that... it's wet. I know that I must be fucked up because I'm aroused by everything he's doing to me.

"You're a fucking dirty little girl, you know that?" he laughs into my ear. "I think you're going to like what I have in store for you."

He removes his hand and picks up the egg again. I watch as it disappears behind my body, closing my eyes and swallowing. He nudges the seam of my pussy with the golden egg, teasing my clit with it.

Nothing, as I expected. The egg is just probing my pussy lips, not easing the ache that I've got in any way. Monster fumbles around on the desk, and then suddenly the egg comes alive with a buzz.

My lips seem dry all of the sudden. My eyes pop open.

That feels... it feels... different. No, it feels...

Good.

As he continues to touch it gently to my clit, I have to suppress a moan. He moves it back and forth, setting a little rhythm, and damn if it isn't hard not to move my hips along with it. The ache I feel increases, spreading outward, but I have too many things to focus on to be mad about that.

Monster pulls the egg away from my clit, nudging my entrance. Though my face is burning with shame, I widen my legs a little, encouraging him to push further. He slides the egg smoothly inside me, just as far as the entrance, and then leaves it there.

He brushes my hair away from my neck and then makes me stand up. After kissing my neck delicately, he nibbles the tender spot just below my ear. When he works his way up to the shell of my earlobe, I cry out, fingers gripping my dress.

"Mmmm," he husks in my ear. "You like that, don't you?"

It's a statement, not really a question. I clamp my mouth shut, trying to pull my dress down around my hips.

"Uh-uh. Who said you could do that?" he asks, swatting my hands away. He unzips his pants, pulling his throbbing pink dick out, and sits down in his chair. "Now get the fuck over here and sit on my lap like a good girl."

"No!" I say, jerking away from his grip. "I'm not going to have sex with you!"

He raises a brow, gripping my arm hard. "First of all, I can fuck who I want, whenever I want. I fucking own you, and I can do whatever the fuck I want to you. Second, I didn't say we were going to fuck. I said, come sit on my lap."

He twists my wrist painfully, and I acquiesce. I perch my ass on his lap, sighing when he releases my wrist. He pulls me further back until my ass cheeks are kissing his long, hard dick.

I've never felt dirtier than at that moment, I swear. He groans as the contact between my ass and his thick penis, holding down my legs with a sprawled hand as he thrusts upward.

I won't lie, it feels kind of good. Kind of taboo and dirty. Like I definitely shouldn't be doing this or letting him do it to me.

Then he ups his game by dipping his hand lower,

searching for my clit. He finds it effortlessly, stroking it lazily. I close my eyes, leaning my head back against his shoulder, breathing in hard.

God, that feels good. It feels like he's filling my body with warmth and fire, just from his simple touch. He thrusts upward against me and kisses the nape of my neck.

Then his free hand shapes my breast through the thin fabric of my shirt, finding my nipple already hard. He pinches it hard, drawing a low groan from my throat.

He chuckles. "You like that?"

I squeeze my eyes shut and turn my head away, but there's no denying it. I like what he's doing. I'm wet, and only getting closer to orgasm. The vibrator buzzes away, Monster thrusts up against me, and his hand starts rubbing my clit faster.

"Oh," I cry softly. "Oh god…"

"That's it, dirty girl. You like how I touch your clit? Or maybe you like the vibrator I put in your pussy? Or is it that you love how I play with your tits?"

His dirty talk just puts me that much closer to the edge. I let out a series of soft little moans, tiny ohs of pleasure.

"I think you'll like it better if you start calling out my name. Go ahead and say it, don't be shy. There can be no secrets between us, Fiore."

His fingers are incessant, strumming my clit or plucking at my breast.

"Oh… oh god…" I call out. "Oh god, Monster…"

I come with a startling series of convulsions, gripping Monster's shoulder for dear life. I feel as if everything is pouring out of me, while at the same time everything is pouring back in. As I ride the wave, Monster holds me down, thrusting up until he roars suddenly.

He pulses his sticky seed onto my ass and my thighs,

groaning quietly afterward. He hits a button on the vibrator's remote, and it stops buzzing. We rest there for almost a minute, our breathing harsh, just trying to get our bearings on the world again.

Then he slides me off his lap. I stand up, my legs wobbly, his cum dripping down my legs. He swats me, and I move forward a few steps.

He stands up, tucks himself back in his pants, and looks at me, seeming bored.

"Give me the vibrator," he says, holding his hand out impatiently.

Shamefacedly, I put my hand down between my legs and fish the egg out. I deposit it in his hand, and he tosses it on the desk carelessly.

"I have work to do," he says. "Close the door on your way out."

I pull my dress back down and skulk out of the office, closing the door behind me. I make it a few steps down the hallway before I mist up, tears overwhelming me, although I can't for the life of me figure out why.

16

KATHERINE

Fiore —

I'll be gone for a few days. In that time, I want you to think very carefully about what you want. It is my suggestion that you sign these papers while I am gone. If not, we'll have to talk about it when I get back. I don't think you want that.

It's not signed or anything. It's just presumed that I will know who it's from, and what he wants.

And I do know, as much as I don't want to.

I read the note again, creasing it when I finish. I found the note on the bed next to me when I woke this morning. Underneath it, there are documents he wants me to sign. It's a contract of sorts, agreeing to give my virginity to him.

Actually, he asks for more than that. He says that by signing the documents, I'd be voluntarily giving up my virginity and the sanctity of my body.

Literally, it says that. The sanctity of my body.

Who would say yes to that? No one in their right mind.

On top of all that, it places the blame for everything — up to and including my abduction — on me.

It's just sheer lunacy.

Incensed, it is everything I can do not to crumple up the note and just throw it in the corner. But I don't. Instead, I seethe quietly over it, pacing in my room and sitting at my window.

I think of what Monster said to me yesterday. I don't believe in taking what isn't mine. That includes your virginity.

When he said he was going to seek other pleasures with me, what exactly did that mean? Somehow, I wasn't foolish enough to believe he just meant he was going to thrust against my ass from time to time.

I lie in my bed, trying to understand. Then I realize that he's a murderer and a kidnapper. Maybe what I am missing here is simply that he's crazy. It does make a kind of sense.

Sick, twisted sense, but still sense nonetheless.

Tired of wallowing in doubt, I gather myself and head downstairs. I bring my book along because *The Count of Monte Cristo* is so poignant to me. When Edmond is incarcerated in the Château d'If, I can feel his pain so acutely, maybe even more than my own.

Wandering around and looking for a spot to read, I find myself in the orchard that my window looks out onto. The cherry blossoms are just beginning to bloom, their tiny blossoms white with the palest hint of pink. There are about a dozen of them, rising proudly against the backdrop of the beige wall.

It's as if they are defiant of their circumstances. This speaks to me too, in its own way.

Heading over to sit under the cherry blossoms, I settle against a comfortable looking trunk. From here, I almost can't see the house at all. It's quiet here too, the grass below me and the trees overhead. It's just a world of white blossoms and knotty, dark brown branches.

I leaf through the pages of my book idly, though I'm not concentrating on the words at all. The words of Monster's letter keep coming back to me, again and again. I can't let them go.

Every time I think of the line *the sanctity of your body*, I go cold with dread. What could that mean?

I drowse here beneath the trees, feeling safe here for some reason. Or safer, anyway.

It's only when I hear footsteps approaching that I wake up, sitting upright. Sin appears through the cherry blossoms, looking relieved when he sees me. He's wearing his usual outfit of black tactical gear.

For some reason, with the trees in blossom as the backdrop, I find that funny. I giggle a little.

He scowls. "You made us look all over the place for you. We thought you were gone."

I cock my head at him. "Would that have been so terrible? There's no way he could've held you responsible."

Sin gives me a sideways look. "I wonder if perhaps we are talking about the same person? Because the man I'm talking about threatened, bullied, and extorted his staff from the very first moment. Perhaps he treats you more kindly."

I'm struck dumb by that for several long moments. "You know that he owns me for sex, right? I'm not exactly here by my own will."

Sin looks down, kicking at the grass. "Yes, I know."

"Okay. Well, just be glad that you're not in my place." I lean back against the tree's trunk with a silent sigh.

Sin glances at me, guilt flashing in his eyes. "Is it bad?"

"What, being forced to... *do things* with him? It's not

ideal." Somehow, I think that Monster wouldn't want me to say any more than that, so I just purse my lips.

Looking behind him as though making sure no one is watching, Sin comes closer and kneels down on the ground. My brows arch as he roots around in the pockets of his tactical vest, producing a simple blue package, smaller than the palm of his hand. He tosses it to me, and I stare at it for a second.

A chocolate bar. He's given me a chocolate bar.

I look up at him, my puzzlement clear. Is this supposed to be some sort of repayment for being Monster's kept toy?

"It's local," Sin says, shrugging a shoulder. "It's really good."

I don't know what it's meant to signify, but I was never one to pass up a treat. Tearing open one end, I inhale the fragrant chocolate. It's dark as sin, almost no milk in it.

I was always one for milk chocolate, but I break off a piece and pop it in my mouth. My eyes almost roll up in my head from the taste of it. It's so very bitter, but still darkly sweet. It makes my mouth water.

When I open my eyes again, Sin is looking at me, just one corner of his mouth crooked upward in a sort of smile. My first thought is that he's really quite handsome, once you get over the cocky bullshit attitude.

"Good?" he asks.

"Yes." I have another little nibble, *mmmm*ing at the taste. Looking at him, I'm curious. "You're not going to being Monster's wrath down on your head by giving me chocolate, are you?"

He lets out a bark of shocked laughter. "Did you just call him Monster?"

I shrug. "It seems appropriate. Besides, I think he likes the nickname."

"Mm. I see. Well, I think that it's okay. You can keep a secret, right?"

His dark eyes twinkle with humor. Nodding slowly, I pass back the chocolate bar. He looks confused.

"I thought you said you liked it."

"I did. But I'm not stupid enough to keep anything that he could find. There would be hell to pay if Monster found out that someone other than him gave me something. *Anything* would probably get you in trouble."

Sin doesn't say anything. He just tucks the chocolate bar back in his vest, sitting down. He looks up for several minutes, seemingly just gazing into the blooms. I'm content to just rest. There's no need for me to speak either.

"Do you sit here because you cannot see the house?" he says at length. He glances at me, his eyes full of a sadness that I can't even begin to ask about.

"Yes." I keep it simple.

He nods. "I can see why. If I were in your shoes, that is."

He glances off into the distance. I'm curious about why he works for Monster. Was he talking about himself when he said that Monster extorted his staff?

The possibility doesn't seem that far off.

But before I can ask, Sin gets up, dusting himself off. "They'll notice I'm gone. I should get back."

I smile at him, tucking my blonde hair back. "You can tell your friends that you found me."

He stares at me for a long moment, seeming about to speak. But at the last moment, he just shakes his head. "Be careful sitting out here by yourself. You never know who is watching and listening."

His warning sends a chill skittering down my spine. I lick my lips, growing anxious. "Thanks."

He turns on his heel, walking away. Soon, he's obscured

by the cherry blossoms, and I have to wonder if he even ever found me at all.

17

KATHERINE

I sit at the bay window in my room, looking out at the faraway mountains. There's a storm rolling in and heavy fog is starting to creep over the hills. It makes me vaguely claustrophobic, but the weather seems to be in step with my mood.

I'm going stir crazy locked up inside this gated fortress. If I don't see the outside soon, I'm really afraid that I'm going to start to lose my mind.

Skulking around the whole property inside the gates, I keep coming to the stables again and again. They are just sitting there, the cedar of the building crisp and new, ready and waiting for someone to explore them. When I first noticed the stables, I figured that they were basically empty, but now I think I was wrong.

I saw an older man hauling a bag of feed into the stables. There's no reason for horse feed unless you have horses. And if there are horses and a stable hand, the equipment to ride must be there too.

But I need a reason to go to the stables, something that

won't make Sin and Monster suspect that I'm trying to escape.

I grind my teeth, trying to think of a solution, but I can only come up with one. There is just no getting around it: I need Monster's permission to get out of this place for a little while.

I spend my afternoon loitering by Monster's office, pretending to leaf through the pages of *The Count of Monte Cristo*. His office door is shut tightly, but I know that he's in there. Trying to seem engrossed in my book, I will him to notice me.

At length, his office door opens. He steps out, looking uncharacteristically sloppy. His dark hair is mussed, his shirtsleeves are rolled up, and his shirt is open at the collar. He looks around and then pins me with his gaze.

"What are you doing here?" he says, scowling.

I sit up, putting my book aside. "Just reading."

His expression turns suspicious. "Bullshit. You can read anywhere, yet you do it in the same hallway as my office? I don't think so. What do you want?"

Drawing a shaky breath, I try another tactic. "You seem stressed. Can I help?"

He leans against the doorway, cracking his knuckles. "Did you sign the papers that I left for you?"

I hesitate. "No."

"Then we have nothing left to talk about. At least, not right now. Believe me, when I am ready to talk about the contract, we will talk."

He starts to go across the hall to his room, but I jump to my feet. "What about a trade? Just because some things are not on the table doesn't mean you have to starve."

He looks surprised. "Are you offering me sexual favors?"

I blush to the roots of my hair, but I lift my chin. "Maybe."

He laughs, the sound deep and melodic. "And what do you want in return?"

Pursing my lips for a second, I blurt out the answer. "I want to go horseback riding."

His brows arch, but I can tell I've got his attention.

"What are you willing to do for such an excursion?" he asks, his expression intense.

I look down at my skinny body, gripping the hem of my dress. "What do you want?"

Monster's gaze narrows. "Your mouth. I want those plump lips wrapped around my cock, moaning as I fill your throat with my cum."

He says it so simply as if his words won't make me blush and stammer. His words are enough to kick my heart into a gallop, enough to make my palms sweaty.

"I... mean..." I say, then I stop and suck in a breath. I can do this. It's in my power. "Deal."

He cocks his head. "All right. Follow me."

He leads me back into his office, waiting until I'm inside before he closes the door. He turns and pins me with a steely grey gaze.

"Have you ever done this before?" he asks, his voice a little rough.

Licking my lips, I shake my head. "No."

The corner of his lips lifts. "Good. Get naked."

"But—"

He grabs my wrist, hauling me up against his firm body. He's hot to the touch. "Do as I say, and everything will be easier for you."

Biting my lip, I pull on my wrist. When he lets me go,

it's simple enough for me to pull the dress I'm wearing off over my head. When I cast it aside, Monster looks pleased.

"That's a good girl," he says, reaching out and touching my breast. He pinches my pouty pink nipple, looking at me for my reaction. I try to keep my face blank, but he tweaks my nipple hard enough that I cry out in pain.

"Get on your knees," he commands, releasing me. He starts to unbuckle his pants, unzipping his fly. He pushes his pants down a little in the front and his dick springs up, thick, and veiny and swollen-looking.

I kneel on the hardwood floor, blushing like crazy when I come face to face with his... *cock*. Monster gives his cock an experimental stroke, motioning me forward with his other hand. I look at it, at the little bead of moisture that forms at the tip, and I realize what a bad plan this all was.

What was I thinking?

"Open your mouth and cover your teeth with your lips," he says, his voice coaxing. "And bring your hand up to brace yourself while you hold my dick. Like this..."

He catches my hands and brings one up to splay across his thigh while the other he places gently around his cock. It's the first time I've ever even touched a penis, so the fact that it's silky smooth surprises me.

So does the fact that it's very warm, and I haven't even started yet.

I glance up at him as I give his cock a long stroke up and down his length as I have seen him do. His eyes are intent on mine and he licks his lips.

"Use your mouth," he says, nudging my lips with his dick. "Just watch those teeth."

I open my mouth, covering my teeth, and hesitantly lower my face to his cock. My tongue cushions his length as I taste the male essence of him, earthy and bitter and salty-sweet all at once. He makes a sound, like he's trying to restrain himself, and looks down at me.

"I only have so much patience. Go faster."

Nervous, I grip his cock harder and go up and down a few times on his length, though there are more than a few inches that I can't take in. He's just too big, too much. He overwhelms my senses; he tastes almost metallic against my tongue.

"Use your hand more," he says, guiding my hand to move up and down his shaft. "Really squeeze it like you mean it but keep pace with your mouth too."

I try to do it all at once, coordinating my hand and my mouth, trying to remember to keep my lips covered. He moans softly while I go down on him, running his hand through my hair. His grip on my hair turns harder, almost painful, right before he loses patience.

"Hold fucking still and keep those teeth covered," he scolds me, grabbing my head with both hands. Monster starts to thrust into my mouth, much harder than I was prepared for.

I gag a little bit each time his cock hits the back of my throat and my eyes start to water. I look up at him, helpless.

"That's it, right there. Fucking perfect," he says as we make eye contact. He punctuates each word with a thrust. "You're a very, very good girl. God, you're going to make me cum, you know that?"

Then his spine stiffens, his eyes rolling back in his head as he thrusts his cock into my mouth. For a second, I can taste the saltiness of his cum before he hisses and pumps it into the back of my throat. I try to breathe through my nose, not fully understanding what has happened.

He slows down, making a satisfied sound. "Ahhhhh."

Only then does Monster pull himself out of my mouth,

leaving me with a bunch of salty semen in my mouth. I swill it around, not knowing what is expected of me now.

He looks at me while he's tucking himself back into his pants. "You'd better swallow that."

He makes it sound like a threat, so I swallow it, my eyes watering again. His cell phone rings, and he moves toward his desk.

"I have business to attend to," he says, seeming distracted.

I open my mouth. "But the deal—"

He walks around his desk, pinning me with his gaze. "I haven't forgotten. Now close the door on your way out."

I climb to my feet, my face red, and I let myself out of his office.

I smile, even as I wipe my mouth. I did it. I conquered one of my goals. There was a power in it, too. A power in saying yes.

That's a good lesson to remember.

And soon, I'll be going horseback riding.

18

KATHERINE

I wake up early, already vibrating with the knowledge that today is the day I get to go horseback riding. I kill a few hours by staring out my window, pretending to flip through the pages of *The Count of Monte Cristo*.

I take a long bath, and then pull a fresh dress on over my head. It's not great riding gear, but I don't care. I get to go out, that's all that matters.

As I'm adjusting the comforter, so all four edges hang neatly off the bed, I'm surprised to see one of the maids come in with an armful of clothing. She dumps it rather unceremoniously on the bed and leaves in a huff.

When I dig through the pile, I find beige riding jodhpurs, a light pink tee shirt, and even a bra and panties. Sitting there, touching satin undergarments, my eyes start to water.

It's been so long since I've worn anything but the simple red shift dress, I don't even know what to do with myself. And of course, when I'm crying, Monster appears.

He's wearing dark riding pants and a navy-blue tee and

looking a little too devastatingly handsome for my tastes. That thought makes me want to blush and cry at the same time.

"You found the clothes then," he says, his face blank. "They're a reward. Be a good girl, and you'll get nice things."

My face crumples, because I'm both very upset by what he's saying and very thankful for the clothes. He looks at me for a second, as if he's trying to determine what exactly he is supposed to do with a crying girl.

"Hurry and get dressed before I change my mind," he says. "I'll be waiting for you in the stables."

He turns on his heel and leaves the room.

Trying not to sob, I change into my clothes, savoring the feeling of satin against my skin. It has been too long since I've worn normal clothes. Too long since I have lived a normal life.

I try to guess how long I've been here.

Weeks? A month? Maybe a little longer? Not much more than that, I think.

After I get dressed, a maid scuttles into my room with a pair of riding boots. Knee high and made of dark leather, their unique scent reminds me of the stables in Audubon Park in New Orleans. Leaning in, I press my face against the cool leather and close my eyes for a second.

For the barest second, I am transported. Back to New Orleans, back in time. A much younger, more innocent version of myself lives there, one whose biggest concern was the fact that her mother had died tragically.

Looking back now, how I long for that kind of life, free from any real worry.

When I have pulled the boots on, I skitter down the stairs, heading for the stables. I find Sin waiting in the yard, and he falls into step with me. He doesn't say anything or show any expression, which I find odd.

"I'm going riding," I say as we cross the lawn. "Monster is taking me."

Sin looks at me with something like reproach. "I'm going too."

"Oh?" I ask. "I guess he wouldn't want me to be without a bodyguard, even here..."

Sin shakes his head. "You're so self-involved. Protecting you is the secondary objective. He's the one with the target on his back."

My eyes widen and my feet slow. "Wait, then why did he agree to take me riding?"

"I wondered the very same thing. I gathered that you had something to do with it." He glowers at me. "Come on, we should get moving."

When we reach the stables, a simple cedar structure, Monster is waiting. The scent of horse manure cloys at my sense of smell, but I don't mind. Like most horse enthusiasts, I learned to love the sweet-bitter scent of the animals long ago.

Monster holds the reins of two sleek black thoroughbreds, his expression indulgent. I walk up to him, my eyes on the horses. They are huge, big enough to crush me with a mere twitch. Using my most gentle voice, I sidle up to the one on the left.

"Hi, sweetness," I murmur, holding my hand out for her to sniff. She snorts, scenting my palm. I lean a little closer, inhaling a lungful of her scent.

"That's an endearment I haven't been called before," Monster says, his mouth kicking up into almost a smile.

I roll my eyes, smoothing my hand over the horse's muzzle. "You wish that I would call you pet names."

He gives me a droll look. "Is this a thing, now? I take you horseback riding, and you give me attitude for it? I'm not sure I like it."

I bite my tongue, switching topics as I pet her neck and shoulder. "What's her name?"

Monster's eyebrows lift. "Her name? I don't know. Sin?"

I look over my shoulder, to where the bodyguard stands. He clears his throat.

"I believe that she is called Reina. The other one is Rey." He shifts his stance, looking uncomfortable.

"Reina," I coo to the horse. "You are beautiful."

She snorts again, nuzzling my palm in search of treats that I don't have. I just pet her instead, lightly scratching her muzzle.

"Alright, I have other things to do, so we should get going. Where is that man who keeps the horses?" Monster asks, looking around behind him.

It takes about fifteen minutes for us to get seated and settled on horseback, Sin included. I notice that Sin is pretty handy at riding, while Monster is stiff and unyielding.

I want to tell Monster that the way he's mounted will cause him a world of pain later, but I don't. Somehow, I don't think that he would take the criticism well and I won't have this ruined for me.

The old man guides us out of the stables, outside the tall fence that runs around the entire mansion. Clinging to my mount, I ride out into a densely forested jungle. There is a stream running somewhere nearby, and there are two paths that have been worn into the jungle, leading opposite directions.

I close my eyes, inhaling. The horse is placid below me, her patience evident. I get a lungful of horse and a hint of the verdant greenery all around me. The world seems to open up to me, and for a minute I am really, truly happy.

Then I am struck by a lightning bolt of sadness because I forgot where I am for a moment. When I open my eyes, I realize that both Monster and Sin are waiting on me. I blush.

"Sorry," I apologize automatically. "I just... I've been cooped up inside the house..."

Monster scowls. "This is your excursion. You've got an hour. Take us somewhere interesting."

My heart starts to race when I realize that he means for me to lead the way. Clucking to Reina, I start off down the path to the right.

The path starts off narrow, so there is only enough room for one horse to proceed at a time. The ground underneath is grassy but there are some rocks hidden here and there.

I keep my horse's pace in check, and she seems to know just how to proceed. She heads down the path, and the green jungle envelopes us. Soon, there is no trace of the stables behind us.

Looking up at the canopy is incredible. As we go down the path, I look around; almost everywhere, I can see some kind of life. Brightly colored birds call out to each other, iguanas, and strange lizards creep along the branches of trees, crickets chirp from everywhere.

The path widens, growing broad enough for two horses. As I rein in my horse, Monster pulls his horse up beside mine. I look at him, giving him a brief smile.

"You ride well," he says, eyeing my posture.

"Oh? You'll have to thank my mother for that. She insisted that I get lessons, even though my father said it was a waste of money."

He cocks a brow. "And he just gave in like that?"

I squint off into the forest. "You didn't know my mother. She was... she could be strong-willed, to put it mildly."

He's quiet for a time. "I was under the impression that you didn't have any female relatives."

What, was I not enough? Would Monster seize the chance to snatch any female relations off the damn street?

My smile falls away. "She died when I was a little girl."

If I expected him to tell me how sorry he is that I have a dead parent, I am to be disappointed. He merely nods, squaring his broad shoulders.

I don't know quite what to say. If ever there was a time to ask him questions about himself, this is it. Silence reigns between us for several minutes, until I speak again.

"Do you just have the one brother, then?" is the best I can come up with.

He slides me a look. "No. I have two brothers, Damen and Dryas."

I absorb that slowly. "Do you all have names that start with D?"

Monster scowls. "No."

"Are you the oldest?" I skirt the issue, trying to keep my tone lighthearted.

"No." He sighs.

"And your family? Do you have a lot of aunts and uncles and cousins?" I am desperate to keep the conversation flowing, and I think that seeps into my tone.

He shakes his head. "Is this an interrogation?"

"No, just... you know, making conversation."

The pointed look he sends my way says that he's not interested in my awkward attempts at being social. Retreating into silence, I feel like a fool. When the path narrows to make it impossible for two of us to ride side by side, I'm relieved.

I drop back and let him take the lead. After all, this is his land.

The sound of water grows louder and louder. The air turns so humid that I can feel it as I ride. Then Monster stops, looking down the path.

Just ahead, there is a small river, its bank all sharp rocks. Monster looks back at me, raising his brows. "Do you want to see it?"

I'm already sliding down off my horse, eager to see anything new and different. What I'm not prepared for is just how rocky the ground is, though.

I stumble and start to fall, looking up at Monster's face. Then I feel a pair of arms wrap me up, enveloping me and helping me find my balance.

Sin is right there, apparently anticipating my fall. I look up at him, feeling a burst of gratitude. When I look back at Monster, his expression has turned foul and black.

I step out of Sin's arms as soon as I can, straightening my spine. Turning to Monster, I put on my brightest smile.

"Ready to see the river?"

As if the moment when Sin caught me was nothing for him to worry about. Which it isn't, but I don't trust Monster to see it that way.

Monster looks between me and Sin. I can almost feel the gears turning, feel him connecting the dots. Just because the dots aren't there doesn't mean anything to a man like Monster.

"You can go," he says to Sin, very slowly. "Go back to the house. Leave us alone."

I move toward Monster, my head held high, determined not to let the moment linger. Hopefully, if I act as if nothing happened, soon enough Monster will decide that it's nothing.

I want very badly to look back, to check on Sin, but I don't. Instead, I just head toward the river.

"Do you think there are like... snakes and crocodiles?" I ask Monster, pulling his attention away from Sin. "God, I hope not. I don't think that these boots are really made for running."

Monster looks toward the river, his hand coming up to the small of my back. "I don't know."

I smile at him, trying to ease our mutual discomfort. All I can do is pray that it worked.

19

ARSEN

"See, the projections for next year are important because..."

The uptight-sounding guy on the call I'm part of drones on. Normally, I don't believe in conference calls. But when someone connected to the Madrigal cartel calls, I can make time for that. They're one of the most powerful cartels in the whole world, and they run the better part of North America.

When they call, I'll listen.

Today, though, they are really disappointing me. I'm one of five big bosses that they're talking to. It looks less and less likely that I'm going to get the contract to distribute all their product in the Southern U.S.

And seeing how the boss that they favor is related to them by blood, there isn't really anything I can do to increase my odds. Aside from murdering mob bosses, that is.

That thought is not off the table, not by a long shot. I crack my knuckles, agitated. The guy is still going on and on about his reasoning behind picking someone related, and I'm about to lose it.

I lean in, interrupting. "So, basically, you are going with the Chicago guys?"

There is a pause on the other end. I look down at my cell phone, sitting next to my laptop. I've made the guy uncomfortable, that's obvious enough.

"It's really all a matter of fiscal responsibility—"

I end the call, incensed. Looking out the window at the courtyard, I try to tamp down the rage, but it just builds and builds inside.

Feelings of impotence and dissatisfaction with myself echo inside my head.

Useless.

Waste of space.

Why do I even try?

Frustrated, I sweep my hands across my desk, sending my laptop and my phone crashing to the floor. But that's not enough for me...

No, I need to take my rage out on a person.

And not just any person. Fiore is front and center in my mind already, taking up too much space in my brain. She's been on my mind the whole time I have tried to work out this deal with the cartel, distracting me.

Detracting from my business, my money.

It's like she didn't *want* me to succeed.

Well, she's about to find out what it means to her, personally, when I don't get my way. My fury is only growing and rising with every moment I wait. Even I know that.

I prowl down the hallway toward her room, single-minded in my determination to reach Fiore. She will have me when I get there; there will be no denying me.

Not anymore. No more pretending like she doesn't want it.

When I reach her bedroom doorway, I find her on her bed, reading. She's lying on her stomach, her legs bent up in the air, a strand of her blonde hair twisted around one of her fingers.

If this were a different world, a different place, she would be an innocent girl just reading a book. But the world is wicked, cruel enough to have put Fiore in the same stratosphere as me.

I wanted her before I ever saw her, desired her screams and moans. Wanted to know how it would feel when I finally took her virginity.

Now, I'm about to find out.

She turns her head to look at me, her eyes widening when she realizes she is not alone. My nickname bubbles to her lips. "Monster?"

Egged on by the thoughts in my own head, I stride toward her. She sits up, folding one foot under her body and tucking a strand of her hair back behind her ear. She looks apprehensive.

"Do you—"

I cut her off, yanking her by the arm up off the bed. I spin her around, raking her hair off her neck, so I can taste her skin there. She locks up, surprised.

"I—" she starts, but I silence her with a growl. I twist one of her arms behind her, keeping her in place with a painful hold. "Ah!"

I bite the nape of her neck and step closer, bringing my big body into contact with her smaller one. The difference between our sizes turns me on, as does the fact that I could ravage her body if I wanted to.

And part of me? Part of me wants to.

Shoving her onto the bed roughly, I start to unbuckle

my belt. She recovers, turning herself over and glaring at me. "What is wrong with you right now?"

I untuck my shirt, my belt still in my hand. "You are my problem, Fiore."

She watches me, her chest rising and falling as she breathes harder. "What is that supposed to mean?"

I grab her ankle, dragging her to the edge of the bed. "Shut the fuck up and get naked."

Doubling the belt, I pull it taut between my hands so that it cracks like a whip. Her eyes track me nervously as she begins pulling her thin dress up over her head.

She reveals miles and miles of creamy, pale skin and taut curves that my hands itch to explore. Better, she's shivering, shaking.

Her nipples are hard, her breasts heaving, her eyes wide. My breath is stolen by the look in her eyes, the terror mixed with lust.

Yeah, she wants this too. Of that, I have no doubt.

She would have me believe that it's all out of fear, but I know the truth. I know that she wants me, almost as badly as I want her.

Considering her for a moment, I play with the belt in my hands. What do I want the most?

Scratch that, I've already answered that enough times. I want everything that she has to give.

But what do I want first?

"Turn over," I say, my words slow and sure. "Get on your hands and knees."

Trembling, looking at me like a bunny would look at a wolf, she moves to face away from me. Fiore kneels down and then gets on her hands, offering me her fucking perfect ass. I move forward, grabbing a handful of her ass.

It's so firm and round, the flesh unmarked, untouched

by any other man. She shivers convulsively as I run my hands down to her thighs, nudging them apart.

Her pussy is revealed to me, as juicy and tempting as a peach. Kneeling on the bed just behind her, I caress her outer lips, frowning in concentration. She turns her head, biting her full bottom lip.

She's trying not to make any sound, trying to pretend like she isn't longing for me to touch her pussy, to find her clit. She doesn't want me to know that she is turned on. But the body doesn't lie...

Just looking at her pussy right now, just stroking the outer lips, I can see her wetness. She can't hide that from me. I'm not interested in whether or not she wants me to know what is so obvious.

Leaning forward, not touching her in any other way, I brush two fingertips over the seam of her pussy, finding her clit. She drops her head low and moans quietly.

The sound of her moaning feeds something deep and dark in my soul. It makes my cock hard, thinking about the noises she's going to make when I fuck her so hard that she can't walk right.

I circle her clit with my two fingertips, enjoying the fact that she leans back to get more. More contact, more friction. Her body is greedy, even though she doesn't understand why yet.

She makes breathy sounds, little ohs of pleasure. I toss the belt aside and move my fingers to her entrance, penetrating her just an inch.

"Oh— oh, oh my God," she whispers. I crane my neck to look at her face and see her clenching her eyes closed. She's hot and slick against my fingers, and I repress a groan.

I make myself take my time, make her want to fuck.

When she wants sex, when she begs me for my cock, it will be worth it.

I withdraw my fingers and push them in again, deeper this time. In and out, deeper each time until my two fingers are in as deep as they'll go. I scissor my fingers inside her, enjoying the strangled sound she makes.

She's creaming all over my fingers, covering my hand. I pull out of her pussy, focusing instead on her clit. She grips the bed and cries out, but I don't let her cum. I keep my strokes lazy.

I need her on the edge of an orgasm, but not quite there. I need her desperate to come, begging for a way to end her suffering. And judging by the way she looks back at me, biting her lip and blushing and trying not to moan, I'm just about there.

"I won't let you finish like this," I tell her, kneading her ass with my free hand. "There's nothing in it for me."

She looks at me, her eyes pleading. "You won't?"

I shake my head. "Nope."

Continuing my lazy strokes around her clit, I slow even more. She makes a frustrated sound.

"Please?" she asks.

"Please what?" I ask, concentrating on her perfect ass.

"Please let me... or make me..." she says, stumbling on the final word. "*You* know."

"Not like this," I repeat.

"Please? I'll... I'll help you..." She moans.

"What? Give me another blowjob?" I slip my fingers into her entrance again, teasing. "While that sounds good, I can think of something much better."

I see the puzzle pieces click into place. "You want..."

"To fuck you? Yes." Pressing my hard cock against her

ass, I make us both moan a little. "I thought that much was obvious."

Her eyes close as I thrust against her ass again. She's growing desperate, just like I wanted.

"You should turn around again, so that I can see your face when I make you come," I say, dropping my voice. "I can touch your tits while I fucking ruin your entire body. You just have to say yes."

I thrust my fingers into her ever so slowly as I push my cock against her ass. She opens her eyes and looks at me. I can see the pain I'm causing written plainly on her face.

She hesitates for a long second, then gives me the barest nod.

Yes. That little movement, her sign of acquiescence, is just what I've been waiting for. I withdraw my fingers from her and step back from the bed, stripping off my shirt and unzipping my pants.

My cock has never been so hard as it is right now, looking down on this girl. Uninterested in waiting for a second longer, I grab her and flip her onto her back, enjoying her wide-eyed innocence.

She gets her first glance at my nude body, at my cock as I push her back onto the bed. I know my body is fucking hard. I know I'm ripped. I know it's impressive to women. There is no reason to hide it, no reason not to bask in the admiration that my huge fucking cock brings me.

Kneeling before her, I part her thighs. I grab her tits for a second, eliciting a little squeak from Fiore's lips. Then I glance down, grasping my cock and positioning it at her entrance. Her ripe, juicy pussy is screaming my name; the blood in my ears is rushing so loudly that I can't hear anything else.

I look at Fiore's beautiful face, at the flush in her cheeks, at the way she bites her lip. Pressing the head of my cock flush against her pussy, I push my cock inside her, just a little. I grit my teeth as her pussy grips my dick.

It's so fucking good.

"Fuck!" she says, breathless and wide-eyed.

I withdraw and thrust again, this time to the hilt. She makes a strangled noise, but she doesn't flinch. Her pussy feels like hot silk, already milking my cock for all it's worth.

"Goddamn," I mutter, trying to set a rhythm. "Fuck, you're so tight. Your pussy is so fucking good, Fiore."

I pump my cock in and out, stroking one of her tits. She practically purrs under the weight of my body, her hand coming up to rest on my back. I move her legs upward, which makes her pussy feel that much tighter. I lean down and nip at her neck, which makes her come off the bed a little.

"Oh," she whispers. "Oh... don't stop..."

I can feel the orgasm rattling around low in my body. If I concentrated on it, I could come within a minute. But I want Fiore to enjoy this too.

Mostly because I want her to know that we only fucked because she agreed to it... but also because I don't want this to be the only time we fuck. I want her waiting on me at the door when I come home, ready to present her pussy to me. I want her to want to get fucked.

So, I lean back and slide my hand down between us, finding her clit. She comes alive when I circle her clit with two fingertips, her nails scoring my back and shoulders.

Hammering into her with my cock, I start to really sweat, my breathing erratic. Fuck, I'm going to come soon. I just need her to finish first.

"Oh... oh... oh, Monster," she pleads, trying to move with me as I thrust. "Just keep doing that..."

I feel her coiling like a snake ready to strike, her pussy contracting in regular time with my thrusts. I pinch her clit, and she goes over the edge, her pussy convulsing and her face euphoric.

I let out a roar, pounding into her body as her tight little pussy wrings every single drop of cum from me. Falling to my elbows, I let my head fall into the hollow of Fiore's neck as I struggle for breath.

Withdrawing my cock gently from her body, I wince at how sensitive my cock is. She sees the expression I'm making and takes it the wrong way.

"You don't have to make that face," she scowls, still breathless.

I roll my eyes, getting up off of her and off of the bed entirely. Looking down, I try to decide if I should wash up in Fiore's bathroom or wait until I get to mine. "Not everything is about you."

She pulls up the comforter around her body, blocking it from my sight. "Will you just go?"

Naked as the day I was born, I lean close to her, grabbing her wrist *hard*. I sneer. "I think you've forgotten who has the power around here. I do, in case you need reminding. What little power you had, you just frittered away because you got a little bit horny."

Her mouth falls open, a perfect picture of shock. I release her, whirling and then storm out of her bedroom. It's better to establish dominance now, just in case she gets any ideas.

A voice in the back of my head, says that I'm weak for even letting her get to me as much as she has. That I was just supposed to use her, ruin her, eviscerate her innocence.

Scowling, I tell that voice to go fuck itself and continue toward my rooms.

20

KATHERINE

Once Monster leaves and I am alone again, I immediately start berating myself for being so weak and stupid as to have slept with him. When he looked at me for that moment of confirmation... when I nodded...

When I came so hard that practically gushed all over his cock, I gave him my permission.

And that little bit of permission was my only damned bargaining chip. Now I am defenseless against him, worse than useless.

Tears well up in my eyes as I think about what I have done. Worse, I've devalued myself.

I feel... defiled. Used. Broken.

Torn apart, in a way that I can never get back.

I get dressed very slowly, blaming myself. Blaming Monster, for being exactly what his name says that he is. Crying over a loss that I can't explain.

Not the loss of my virginity, because that isn't anything to mourn. But the loss of my freedom. My happiness. My whole life in New Orleans.

Gone, gone, gone.

I lie in my bed, my comforter pulled up around my neck. I try to calm myself, closing my eyes. I must fall asleep because when I open my eyes again, I see Sin's face. He's shaking me.

"Wake up," he whispers, looking over his shoulder.

"Why are you—"

He stops my words by putting his fingers against my mouth. "Sssshhhh."

Sitting up, I try to shake off my sleeping state. Sin looks around, spying my open bathroom door. He motions for me to be quiet, then heads to the bathroom. I follow on silent feet, insanely curious as to what exactly is going on.

He seals us inside the bathroom, but he still speaks so low that I almost can't hear him. He gets right up next to my ear, whispering.

"You still want to leave?"

I pull back, running a hand through my blonde hair. "Why?"

Sin looks aggravated. "Yes or no?"

"Of course, I do—"

"Keep your voice down!" he whispers, glancing at the door behind him. "Jesus fucking Christ! Do you want us to get caught or something?"

Staring at him for several long seconds, I try to piece everything together. "You're saying..."

"I heard him talking. He's gonna fire me and replace me with someone you're not attracted to, or some crazy shit."

"And?" I say, hopeful.

"And this is likely my last chance to get you out of the house."

He's not expecting how fast and hard I hug him, judging from the sound he makes. "*Oof.*"

Tears prick my eyes, happy tears. I haven't let myself

imagine escape very many times since that first time, but now...

Sin pushes me off. "No crying. We don't have that kind of time."

Sniffling and wiping at my nose with the back of my wrists, I nod. "Okay. Do you have a plan?"

He looks very intense. "Yeah. Well, sort of. It's not what I would call really solid, but... it'll do."

Anxiety races up my spine. "What is it?"

"He's leaving for the airport soon. I'm supposed to drive into town to pick up some supplies shortly after he leaves. I think the best bet would be for you to hide in the trunk of the car. That way, I can smuggle you out without anyone looking for you. No one will think to check my trunk."

He sounds more confident than his expression indicates. I narrow my gaze.

"What if it doesn't work?"

"What if it does?"

Sighing, I turn to pace on the bathroom floor. "If it doesn't work, if we get caught... I mean, he will kill us both. Literally. He already suspects some kind of affection between us..."

Sin glowers, cracking his knuckles. "He suspects more than that. He questioned my men about our relationship."

For a second, I waste time being upset that Monster would even think that there was a relationship between me and Sin. How could there ever be, when all the air in every room I've been in since I got here is sucked up by Monster?

I take a deep breath to steady myself. "When do you think we should go?"

He looks at his watch. "It's three thirty. He's supposed to leave at four. I think it would be best if we got you out into the car now before everybody starts to wake up."

My stomach drops. "Right now?"

"Yep. I think that it's our best shot. Our only one, assuming that you really want out of here."

My heart squeezes. "Of course, I want out."

"Well... let's go. If we go down to the front gate, the cars should already be parked there, ready and waiting."

The silence stretches between us for a second as I try to still my racing heart. "Can I just... have just a minute in here, alone?"

Sin raises his brows but inclines his head. He quietly lets himself out of the bathroom, and I close the door behind him. As I quickly use the restroom, I try to wrap my mind around the fact that I am actually on the verge of escaping.

My freedom, something I thought was gone forever, is suddenly and inexplicably within my reach. Instead of worry about what Monster wants or what Monster thinks, I might soon be able to think about what I want. What *I* think.

I laugh quietly to myself, the first fit of humor since I arrived here. How fitting that it should be in the moment I leave.

Then I let myself out of the bathroom, moving on silent feet. Sin waits for me, keeping watch at the bedroom doorway.

"Ready?" he mouths. I nod, trying not to be too fearful.

After I leave this room, though, there is no going back. And if I flee, I'll be running for my life.

Gripping the hem of my dress anxiously, I follow Sin out of the bedroom and down the darkened hallways. The house is hushed at this hour and everything is shut down. My footsteps seem loud; by comparison, Sin's booted feet sound quiet. As he leads me around corners and down the back stairway, I swear my heart is so noisy in my own ears that I am genuinely worried it might draw attention to our passage.

I keep thinking what Monster is doing right now. What if he comes to the part of the house where we are sneaking through? It would be an anomaly, sure, but it's not impossible.

In the back of my mind, I am already cringing at the thought of what he will do and say if he finds us. Already preparing for the moment of truth, I can't stop picturing both of us kneeling on the ground as Monster stands before us, looking particularly deadly.

I know what men like my father call shooting someone point blank to the head. *Execution style.*

The knowledge is like a lump of cold hard coal solidifying in the pit of my stomach. As I follow Sin down the final flight of stairs, I can't help the tremors that make my hands shake. Sin stops on the bottom step, holding up his hand. I take that to mean I should stop.

He turns still as stone, listening intently. Long seconds tick by, without me having a clue what he hears. I just stand behind him, hoping and praying that Monster isn't about to come around the corner.

Then Sin starts moving again, waving me forward into the ill-lit hallway. We turn a corner, and Sin tugs me toward the mansion's front door. For some reason, that in itself causes me anxiety.

I've never been through the front door. I've never had any reason to do so, to be honest.

He creeps along stealthily, and I follow him around several corners. Then, at last, we are at the front door, and he gives me the gesture to wait again.

He slinks forward to the actual door, as elegant as a

panther. The door has a large plate glass window in the middle, and Sin peers out of it.

I do my best to wait silently, even though I am shivering so violently that you can actually hear my teeth chatter. To my right, the grand staircase rises upstairs. All around, there are hardwood floors and bland beige walls. I try to count the floorboards, to calm myself down.

Again, Sin is still and quiet. Again, the waiting seems to take forever, though it couldn't have been more than a minute.

Then he's apparently satisfied because Sin swiftly moves to open the door. In my head, I was prepared for an alarm to start shrieking, but of course, it doesn't.

No need to set an alarm on a door when you have a team of private security guys on hand to guard your whole property.

Sin pulls the door wide, motioning me forward. I hesitate and then walk out of the doorway. I look down at the cars, parked a hundred yards away from where I stand. Two Mercedes-Benzes, both perfectly white as if to match the house.

The front yard is perfectly still and quiet. I look up at the mountainous areas that I know are splayed out all around the house. I can feel something. Or sense something.

I motion to Sin to wait, but he emphatically shakes his head. He encourages me to move forward, his eyes roving, ever vigilant. He grabs me by the arm, jerking me forward, and we go down a few steps.

To our right, I can see the broad clay steps that lead around back. To the left, I can see the edge of the stables. Sin propels me straight ahead, fishing the keys to the Benz out of his tactical vest.

Again, there is something that is off about everything,

some little sense of wrongness. But I let Sin hurry me around to the back of the car, where he pops the trunk. I hesitate again only a couple of feet away from the car.

This just feels wrong. Sin pushes me roughly toward the trunk.

"Get in," he whispers harshly. "Right now, before—"

Then all hell breaks loose. A bullet zings through the air, missing Sin by mere inches. He crouches and moves closer to the Benz trying to figure out where the gunfire came from.

"Shit," I hear him mutter.

Large lights come up on the lawn, illuminating it. I hear men running down the steps leading from the backyard. I peek around the car and see that Sin is between them and me.

I bet they've been told not to shoot me. At least, I hope so…

My heart pounding, I take off in the opposite direction, toward the stables. The men behind me are yelling in Spanish, but I can understand their meaning well enough.

Get her!

I sprint for the stables, my arms and legs pumping, my brain struggling to compute. Out of the corner of my eye, I catch a glimpse of Monster from afar. He's coming down the front stairs, not even looking at me yet.

Yes, there may be a chance yet.

If I can just get into the forest, past the stables… I might be able to escape still.

Gritting my teeth, I haul myself toward the stables, running flat out.

21

ARSEN

I've known about Fiore and Sin's little flirtation for days. Weeks, actually. I should have realized the first time I saw the connection there in her eyes. I should have fired him.

Fuck, I should have killed him just for looking at what is mine.

Instead, I'm racing across the front lawn at a ridiculously early hour in the morning, where several of my guards have captured Sin. I pull my gun out of the back of my pants, holding it at the ready. He's sputtering in Spanish, telling his men that they should be attacking me. Yelling about loyalty, or some shit.

But Sin should know that these men value the price of gold above loyalty. He is one of them after all, mercenaries down to a man. My antennae went up a few days ago, and then I had a private talk with each of his men.

Ergo, they became my men.

"Where the fuck is she?" I demand, pointing the gun directly at him. "Huh? Where's that little cheating slut? Tell me, and I won't put a bullet in your brain right now."

He doesn't speak, but he does glance nervously toward the stables. I turn my head, and I catch a glimpse of blood red vanishing through the stables.

"You're fucking stupid," I tell Sin. I spit on the ground near him. "She may just be a whore, but you're not fucking good enough for her."

"It's not what you think—" he says, moving to stand.

I look him right in the eye and put a bullet in his head. He groans for a second, then he slumps backward, dead. I would've liked to spend a little more time on him, to really teach him a lesson about how traitors get treated.

But I have a girl to hunt down. Priorities, priorities.

"Get the four wheelers," I say to the Columbian standing next to me. "I bet she went down the trail behind the stables."

"Sir," he says, setting off at a jog.

I race toward the stables too, my mind oddly clear. Fiore is the foremost thing on my mind at the moment. Finding her. Bringing her back.

Punishing her.

I'm cool as I make it through the cedar stables. Calm as I climb on one of the four wheelers. Collected as I race the vehicle down the path.

It's dark in this forest at this early hour, really dark. For a few seconds, it's just me and the forest. I start to worry that maybe I was wrong, maybe she took a different path, maybe...

The sound of the river grows louder and louder. I am almost about to admit defeat, to turn the vehicle around and head back.

And then I see a flash of the blood red dress. I can just make her out, running ahead of me. She has veered off the path, running toward the river.

She's smart if she planned that. I can't make it very far off the path, so I have to continue down to the rocky river bank. Racing down to where the water flows, I stop the engine, leaving the four-wheeler idling, and race down the river bank. I can see her now, only a few hundred yards off, her long blonde hair flying wildly behind her.

I chase her because it's the only thing I know how to do.

Fiore's pale arms and legs move in a blur. I notice her slow a little, limping. It occurs to me that while I might be running this rocky shore in my boots, she is barefoot.

The river gets louder and louder, which must mean that there will be a waterfall somewhere soon. She, apparently, finds that out too because she stops suddenly, looking back at me.

I grin. I've won, she just doesn't know it yet. Because she has three options...

One, to keep running to the left. Eventually, a combination of my guards, her bare feet, and my sheer physical strength will just wear her down. She'll fall, I'll catch her, and I'll win.

Two, she can jump. Judging by the waterfalls I've seen around here, she would be forfeiting her life. In that case, I win too.

Third, she just gives up now. And then... surprise, surprise. I win, again.

My grin is still in place as I jog up to her. She's staring at the ground beyond where the earth falls away, trying to measure the distance.

"Don't jump," I call out, a little out of breath. "Or do. But don't do it on my account. A dead slave is no good to me."

I can see the whites of her eyes, standing out in the dim light. The look on her face, like she can't believe where she is right now. A lone tear tracks down her face, and she makes no move to try to remove it.

She glances away, over the falls again. She's out of choices. Out of time.

"Fuck you," she whispers. "You did this to me. You brought me to this point, right now."

"No one said that I was going to treat you well," I say with a shrug, walking toward her.

"Stop!" she orders, but I don't. There's only me and her now, me and her and that steep drop.

"Come back now, and we can talk about your punishment—"

A second before she jumps, she sneers at me. That look, her blue eyes pinning me... it travels right through me like I'm nothing.

Then she jumps or rather lets herself fall. She goes over the edge suddenly, disappears with a shriek.

I'm at a loss for words.

What the fuck?

I head to the edge, looking way down into the foamy black water. It swirls and gushes as if nothing ever happened.

Around me, the forest sounds fade away, and I can only hear the river and the sound of my own heartbeat.

GET A FREE BOOK!

Join my mailing list to be the first to know of new releases, free books, special prices and other author giveaways.

http://freehotcontemporary.com

ALSO BY JESSA JAMES

Bad Boy Billionaires
Lip Service

Rock Me

Lumber Jacked

Baby Daddy

Billionaire Box Set 1-4

The Virgin Pact
The Teacher and the Virgin

His Virgin Nanny

His Dirty Virgin

Club V
Unravel

Undone

Uncover

Cowboy Romance
How To Love A Cowboy

How To Hold A Cowboy

Beg Me

Valentine Ever After

Covet/Crave

Kiss Me Again

Handy

Bad Behavior

Bad Reputation

Dr. Hottie

Hot as Hell

Pretend I'm Yours

Rock Star

ABOUT THE AUTHOR

Jessa James grew up on the East Coast but always suffered a severe case of wanderlust. She's lived in six states, had a variety of jobs and always comes back to her first true love – writing. Jessa works full time as a writer, eats too much dark chocolate, has an iced-coffee and Cheetos addiction, and can't get enough of sexy alpha males who know exactly what they want – and aren't afraid to say it. Dominant, alpha-male insta-luv is her favorite to read (and write).

Sign up HERE for Jessa's Newsletter:

http://jessajamesauthor.com/mailing-list/

Follow me on BookBub:

www.ingramcontent.com/pod-product-compliance
Lightning Source LLC
La Vergne TN
LVHW011832060526
838200LV00053B/3985